WHEN A LIONESS GROWLS

A LION'S PRIDE #7

EVE LANGLAIS

CHAPTER ONE

"PLAY IT AGAIN." Because once just wasn't enough for them to truly understand what they saw.

Without saying a word, Arik, the lion pride king, his expression quite serious, replayed the video on the large screen. For a moment, utter silence reigned, a rarity when more than a few of the pride were gathered.

The grainy film, shot in shades of green—the taping done at night via a special filter—showed a clearing in a jungle, or so the broad-leafed foliage would indicate. Into the opening ran a woman with long flowing hair dressed in a bikini with only a filmy wrap to cover it.

The woman on screen glanced over her shoulder, her features facing the camera, consternation clear on her face. Her bosom noticeably heaved. It was a mighty bosom. Stacey's more modest bosom hated it on principle.

A blur of movement at the edge of the screen and another figure moved into view. Definitely male in build and stature, but not entirely human.

"What the fuck is it?" asked the ever-eloquent Luna.

"It looks just like a minotaur," observed Melly with a cant of her head, as if turning it sideways would clarify matters.

"But with a lion head. Totally cool," added Meena.

"The loin cloth is a nice touch." Stacey noticed things like fashion.

"I've never heard of a minotaur with a lion head." Noted with clear confusion.

"On account minotaurs specifically have bull heads."

"But do they have bull-sized balls?"

"Does it fucking matter?" Luna snapped. "It's obviously not a bull head, therefore not a minotaur."

"What should we call it then? A liotaur?" Joan tossed in her two cents.

The shouts of "Brilliant", and the high-fives aimed at Joan, some of them slapping harder than necessary, solved the question of what to call the man on the screen but still didn't answer any questions.

"Is it real or a hoax?" asked Teena, who had to stand since the chair she'd tried to sit in unexpectedly collapsed.

Arik shrugged. "No idea. The footage isn't clear enough to tell if it's a mask or not. I will, however, note that I've never seen or heard of a species with only a lion's head before." Technically, any shifter with enough control could do it, but why only settle for the head when four legs with a tail was so much more awesome?

Raising the remote, Arik pressed a button and replayed the video again, slower this time, frame by frame, so the group could lean close and take in every detail.

The ladies that made up the crew of Baddest Biatches—now superheroes courtesy of some zombie ass-kicking caught the previous month on video—sat around mulling the footage and what it meant.

No surprise, they couldn't contain their curiosity.

"What do you think happens after he carries her off?" Joan mused aloud.

"I'd say that's pretty obvious. What else does a man want a woman for?" muttered Luna with a good dose of sarcasm. "Or should I draw a picture for you?"

"Oh hell no. Not with the pictures again." Reba's nose wrinkled. "Your artistic skills leave much to be desired."

"What are you talking about? I am an excellent artist."

"Of stick people and squiggles."

"Maybe if you had some imagination you would understand talent," Luna growled.

"If you call that talent, then I'm an excellent singer."

"How about we focus on the video and not your monthly tournament of Win, Lose, or Claw?" suggest Arik.

"I think we should address it because she and her stick people keep making us lose," Joan accused with a pointing finger.

"Put it away or I'll tear it off."

"I'd like to see you try," said Joan with a smirk.

Luna stood, every inch of her bristling.

"Enough," roared Arik.

The squabbling women quieted, but Luna indicated with a tilt of her head that she and Joan would continue the discussion outside. Joan smiled. A Bad Biatch never walked away from a battle—unless she just had her nails done and the French manicure had cost a fortune. Then, a woman might choose to focus on what their king was trying to impart.

"Is that the entire video?" Stacey asked.

"Yes. And before you ask, it arrived anonymously with only a sheet of paper." Arik held up the empty white parchment, whose letterhead read simply: Club Lyon Resort.

"Isn't that resort one of ours?" Stacey asked.

"It is indeed. Club Lyon was acquired by the pride's corporation. After extensive renovation, it finally opened thirteen months ago."

Luna frowned. "Hold on a second. If this happened on a pride-owned property, how come we're hearing about this anonymously?"

"That is a very good question. One that needs an answer."

"I know the answer." Melly's hand shot up. "No one wanted to tell the boss because they were afraid he'd kick their ass."

"That is a distinct possibility. And one that I will address. However, this abduction situation also needs to be looked into. Once I received this video, I had Leo do some digging."

"That's my pookie," Meena exclaimed. "Always with his books and research. He's so smart and hot."

Someone made a gagging noise. "Would you stop it already? We get that he's taken. No need to shove our faces in it."

"It's always good to remind you single gals that he's mine, and you all remember what happened to the last girl who tried to touch him." That girl ended up in traction and bald. The most unnerving part of the attack? Meena did it with a smile.

"Back on track, ladies." Arik snapped his fingers and earned a few snickers, probably because he'd called them ladies.

Stacey flicked her hair back over her shoulder. Only one real lady in this room.

"What did Leo find?" Luna asked.

"It appears women have been disappearing in and around the island for over a year now," Arik noted, pointing to a folder on the table. "In most cases, the women are found, safe and sound, a few days later, with no memory of where they've been. It gets chalked up to an island adventure that got a little wild. No big deal usually except this seems to be happening almost exclusively from our resort, and we have this." He pointed to the screen and indicated the paused image of the liotaur.

"You say the resort never reported anyone as missing. How do we know she was even staying there?"

"Right after I docked them all for negligence, Leo accessed their database and confirmed she was a guest."

"Is she human or shifter?" asked Melly.

"Shania Korgunsen is twenty-three years old and is of mixed blood but non-shifting." Which meant one human parent, one shifter parent. Even if unable to transform, the girl would be a carrier of the gene.

"How long since she disappeared?" Luna asked.

"Room records show Ms. Korgunsen has not been to her room in two days." Arik slammed the table. "Two freaking days and no one reported it to me, and by all indications, no one has been able to find any trace of her."

5

"Don't we have any trackers at the resort?" Reba asked. Her nose wrinkled. "Surely someone out there has a nose to pick up the tracks."

"You would think that someone could find something, but because of a heavy rain shower, we can't even confirm Ms. Korgunsen was in that clearing, despite the visual evidence."

"And you're sure no one has seen or heard from her since she was kidnapped?"

"Maybe she's dead." Melly, their resident B-grade-horror-movie geek, drew a line across her throat. "Shredded to pieces during the throes of his passion."

Joan snorted. "Or maybe she loved it so much she chose to stay with leo-dude."

"Either way it doesn't matter. I won't have this happening. Our reputation, and even our secret, is at risk. If someone is abducting women, then I want it stopped, and I want the names of those covering it up." Arik almost roared, and the Baddest Biatches took note of their king's demand.

A dangerous mission in paradise? A hot dude and a mystery?

The volunteers were quick to shoot hands in the air, screaming, "Me, I'll do it."

Fights also immediately broke out.

Luna lunged across the table in order to muffle Reba, shouting, "She can't go. She promised to handle the visiting bear contingent next week."

To which Reba replied, "Luna can't go either on account she's pregnant!"

Luna's mouth rounded into an O of shock. "You bitch! That was supposed to be a secret."

"As if you could hide your widening ass."

"You're just jealous because I have an ass."

"I'll do it!" Joan offered.

At this, Melly shot her cousin a glare. "You are not leaving me here alone to deal with Grandmother while Mom is on a cruise."

"She loves you."

"Last time I checked in on her she made me trim her claws—with my teeth!"

As they all argued their merits, Stacey shook her head. None of them were going because she had them all beat. She closed the file that she'd snared while everyone yapped and yodeled.

She raised her hand, and her very politeness had the lionesses quieting as Arik said, "You wanted to add something, Stacey?"

"There is only one obvious choice for this mission. Whatever is happening over there requires a certain finesse. And attributes." She fluffed her fiery locks.

"Are you saying he likes redheads? Easy enough to dye mine," Joan replied.

"Until you drop your pants and the rug below doesn't match," retorted Luna.

"Shaving would take care of that."

"I'm not speaking of hair," Stacey muttered. "But access. I can get into places most of you can't."

"I'm capable of taking one for the team," Joan said with a wink.

"She's not talking about sex," Reba snapped. "I know what she's talking about and so do you. You just don't want to admit she's best suited for this job."

"How is she supposed to handle a possible predatory abductor? She's only an event specialist," Joan argued.

"Only?" Stacey arched a perfectly groomed brow. "I'll have you know that my job is very complex. And that same job will get me into offices and access to people that a regular guest might not have."

"Because telling them you're planning a wedding or bachelorette party is going to lead you to a kidnapper." Joan rolled her eyes.

"What if it does?"

"How will you handle it? Threaten him with the mascara in your purse?"

"Nothing wrong with looking good. You should try it sometime," Stacey remarked with a disparaging glance at Joan, still dressed in her running attire.

"Don't knock Stacey's skills. She is a member of the Baddest Biatches for a reason," Reba stated, coming to her defense.

Arik held up his hand. "Enough. With event coordinator status within the pride, Stacey could totally gain access to places if they thought she was there to plan a huge event," Arik mused aloud. "It's settled. She is going."

Stacey's lips curved in triumph.

Her victory was short-lived. "I don't want you going alone." The king sounded most adamant on that point.

"Must I take one of them?" she said with a melodramatic sigh. Faked of course. If one lioness in paradise was fun, a pair of them together meant trouble with a capital T.

"Take one of the crew and cause another international incident?" Arik laughed. Laughed for a good minute. "I think not. Not to mention sending you with any kind of male lion might spook the target. We need someone a bit more under the radar."

"Is Jeoff going to loan me a puppy?" Jeoff, as head of the small city wolf pack, also doubled as pride security. She could handle a wolf. Get it a nice leash and collar, bedazzled of course, for when she took it on walks.

"Actually, I've got something better than a wolf in mind."

And by better he meant tall, handsome, and utterly repressed.

The mission kept getting better and better. Especially since Arik handed her—albeit unknowingly—the pride's credit card to shop for some clothes so she'd fit in. *I am going to paradise.* Which meant she needed a teeny-tiny bikini—the smaller, the better—plus loads of sunscreen because her fair skin would burn. Good thing Arik gave her a partner to slather it on.

Rawr.

CHAPTER TWO

THIS MISSION SUCKED BALLS ALREADY. Surely he could be doing something better with his time. Anything. Even watching paint dry sounded more fun. But no, Jean Francois was being a good soldier for his boss.

"I need you to deliver something safely." That was the only instruction the boss gave JF, other than telling him to wait on the airstrip outside town. An airstrip owned by the local lion's pride. *Don't tell me we're doing another favor for those mangy felines.*

Ever since they'd come to town, the local pride had been a source of annoyance. Who decided it was a good idea to give household pets such a commanding role? And why did his boss, Gaston, feel such a need to cater to this supposed lion king?

Ever since Gaston had hooked up with that feline Reba, the boss had been doing all kinds of things that were out of character, including smiling. A necromancer smiling, and sometimes even laughing. With joy.

Ugh. What was it about love and happiness that took a great man like Gaston and made him weak? Soft. So soft that his boss thought he should send his right-hand man on a stupid mission that involved waiting.

And more waiting, as the appointed time of eight a.m. came and went. If JF were a less patient man, he would have left, but the boss paid for his smartphone data, so he contented himself watching an episode of *Breaking Bad* on Netflix.

At about half past ten, a sports car, painted a bright cherry red, which, surprisingly enough, didn't come with a trail of screaming cop cars, screeched to a halt outside the plane. A curvy redhead in an outfit that should never see the light of day—the dress more suited as a shirt, given how much leg it exposed—popped out of the front seat, holding aloft a box.

At last. The package for delivery. About time.

Exiting his car, he took long strides towards her. "I'll take that." He held out a hand for the box and couldn't help but note just how big he was in comparison to the woman, something that didn't daunt her at all.

The darkness inside him took note of her scent—feline, no surprise, but with a hint of cinnamon spice. The aroma of her wrapped around him and made his mouth water for a bite.

No eating the messenger. Given her red hair, she'd probably be the type to get angry while he ate.

"Aren't you just a dollface. Thank you." She beamed as she handed the package to him. His arms dropped at the weight.

"What the hell is in this thing? Rocks? A dead body?" One never knew with his boss, and given the woman belonged to the lion pride, a crazy fucking bunch, for all he knew it contained a bomb.

"I can't tell you. It's a secret. All I can say is I need it."

"Need it for what?" he asked as she skipped toward the outside set of stairs leading up to the open door of the plane.

"We'll need it for our trip to the tropics."

We? Surely he misunderstood. "Our?"

"Didn't Gaston tell you? You're coming with me."

She was the package? "There must be a mistake."

"No mistake, sweetcheeks. Once you store that box on board, don't forget to grab my luggage in the trunk."

"I think there's been a mistake." He repeated the words. "No one said anything about a trip." Surely Gaston didn't hate him that much. He'd bet this was the work of his boss's new girlfriend. Trying to get him out of the picture by sending him away with one of her cat friends. *Do I look like a pet sitter?*

The feline in question didn't seem to notice his reluctance. She paused in the doorway of the plane, one foot, encased in a ridiculously high heel, sitting on the top step, a vibrant sight in a bright yellow dress that drew his eye—and a red pinprick of light from a laser sight.

Bang.

The shot missed, and not because JF moved lightning quick. The redhead saved herself. One moment a woman stood on the ramp, and the next second, clothes hit the ground and she was soaring, and snarling, hands extended and shifting into paws. When she hit the pavement, she bounded in the direction of the gunshot.

Bang. Bang. The shooter hiding behind a car parked outside the fencing bordering the airstrip kept shooting, and missing. The lioness dodged each shot and kept going.

Great. Just fucking great. Want to bet this incident would create some paperwork? Not to mention cleanup. The only saving grace was the incident—and by incident he meant her shifting into lion form and not the shooting —was done in a rather remote location. Still, though, he'd probably have to take care of witnesses.

A slam of a car door and a squeal of tires made it clear they wouldn't catch the shooter. While she sprinted after it, JF didn't. He wasn't about to chase after the vehicle like some common canine.

So once more, JF waited, but he didn't wait silently. He put in a call to his boss. It rang four times and went to voicemail.

He dialed again.

And again.

The line was answered with a snapped, "What is so important it couldn't wait?" Gaston sounded out of breath. Did he and his girlfriend ever get out of bed these days?

"You cannot seriously expect me to travel with one of those lunatic felines." JF didn't bother to hide his disdain. He had no patience for shifters, not after what they'd done to him.

"I take it you've met the package." A hint of a smirk in the tone.

"Yes, I've met her. She's off right now chasing a car."

"And you let her?"

"I didn't realize I was supposed to stop her. Perhaps some warning would have helped. Then I could have brought a can of tuna to keep her occupied."

"I gave you an order to protect the package."

"And I did. I'm holding it in my hand."

"I meant Stacey."

"Package implies non-living creature. Not a woman." A very sexy woman who roared her annoyance as taillights winked out of sight.

"It doesn't matter what she is. It is your duty to ensure Stacey remains intact while she investigates an issue."

Stacey, a woman he'd seen a few times since his arrival in town. A woman he did his best to avoid.

"Does this issue she's investigating have anything to do with why someone was at the airstrip waiting to shoot her?"

"Someone attacked?" Gaston sounded surprised.

"Why do you think she chased that car?" Which made him wonder for a moment if the boss's girlfriend chased cars just for fun.

"A shooting on pride turf. How brazen and peculiar. And unacceptable. You were supposed to keep her safe."

"She's alive, and perhaps I would have known to expect violence if you'd told me something about the fucking job."

"I expect better from you, JF. I promised the lion king you'd keep his serf safe during her travels."

"The only way to keep a crazy lion safe is by putting them in a cage." They had no common sense. They also attacked without provocation. The memory of his wounds no longer had the power to make him flinch.

"No caging the woman, JF. Or tying her up. Or restraining her in any way. You are to assist her in whatever way she needs."

"I'd rather not."

"But you will." Gaston sounded quite firm on this point. "Be sure to report back daily. I want to know what you find once you arrive at your destination."

"You seriously expect me to travel with her."

"Now more than ever. I want answers to the mystery."

"What mystery?"

"Ask Stacey." With those cryptic words, his boss hung up. Redialing would have to wait because from the shadows sauntered a large feline, her fur tinged with auburn, her tail standing tall and snapping with pride.

The large cat stopped by the trunk, cocked her head, and roared at him.

"Did you just give me shit?"

"Rawr."

"Stop your caterwauling and get on the plane. We're late."

At that rebuke, the cat stiffened then softened, the lines of her shape blurring until a woman stood there. A naked woman with full hips and strawberry-colored nipples. The fiery mane on her head matched the carpet below. As a man, it was his duty to notice such things. He also noticed she looked good enough to eat, and his fangs pressed into his lips, hunger wakening in him and tempting him for a bite.

She's not food. A part of him knew that, and yet he still stared in a very ungentlemanly fashion. She did nothing to stop him. Her lips curved in a smile, and her hip tilted ever so slightly.

"Get a good peek?" She winked. "Be a good boy and maybe I'll introduce you to the mile-high club."

He knew she tried to shock him. Women like her seemed to make a game of it. But Jean Francois wasn't new to this game. He turned his back on her and stated, quite distinctly, "Sex on a plane is nothing. Try doing it outside in the clouds without a safety net."

Yeah, he dared her. And then walked away.

CHAPTER THREE

STACEY GAPED after the man as he headed into the small plane with the box she'd given him. She still stared as he exited empty-handed and clomped down the stairs.

"Are you going to stand there all night, or are we leaving?" he barked. "And where is the pilot?"

"The pilot is coming, sweetcheeks." A nickname he'd earned because of the way it made a tiny muscle jump high on his cheek. She popped open the trunk and leaned over. On purpose of course. "Give me a moment to grab a new outfit before you stow my bags."

She unzipped her case and shoved her hand inside, fingers brushing silken fabric. She tugged a dress free, the loose texture and bright color a perfect foil for her hair and the climate they would be visiting.

Straightening, she noted him right behind her, his expression carved in granite, looking so serious, and yet, he couldn't hide the spark of red in the depths of his eyes. His inhuman eyes.

The red spark was part of his heritage as a whampyr,

17

a creature only recently discovered when a bunch of them came to town with an honest-to-goodness necromancer. Lucky Reba had snared that fine catch.

What exactly was a whampyr? No one knew for sure, and Gaston, their master, wasn't telling. Stacey and the others only knew the basics. Some kind of shapeshifter, with a body that resembled that of a gargoyle crossed with a bat. For their diet, they drank blood, and yet, according to Gaston the necromancer, they weren't vampires. And that was all he'd say.

A secret. Stacey liked secrets, which was why this mission to the Caribbean excited her.

It took only a moment for Stacey to yank the dress over her body. It fell in pleats that showcased her shape. "Hand me my shoes." She pointed to them lying on the ground, having fallen during her shift.

"Get them yourself."

Someone was ornery in the morning. Was it because the sun hurt his skin? He kept himself pretty well covered, wearing a pair of linen slacks, a long-sleeve shirt, and a jacket. But no tie. He also sported a short-trimmed beard.

Friction for the thighs. How thoughtful.

"I don't think we've had the pleasure of meeting in person before. My name is Stacey Smithson."

"I don't really care."

"What an odd name to give you."

He glared so she laughed.

"While you might say you're not interested, I know better, sweetcheeks. You've been eye-balling me for a while." Just like she'd eyed him.

"If you saw me looking, it was only to ensure you

didn't turn rabid and attack me. Your kind isn't known for being too stable."

Her smile widened. "You say the most darling things. I will say I am most excited you've been chosen to come along as my bodyguard on this trip."

"As if anything could guard you from your own insanity."

"True." How well he knew her already. "But I will enjoy watching you try. You're an intriguing creature, Jean Francois Belanger. I look forward to finding out how you came to work for Gaston Charlemagne."

"I might not be employed by him for long. Given his recent orders, I am thinking of updating my resume." Said utterly straight-faced.

But she could tell he was having fun. Just look at the muscle jumping in his cheek. "You should apply to work for the pride. We have great dental benefits."

"I'd rather shoot myself first."

"Aren't you just a ray of sunshine. I can see we'll have so much fun together."

"No, we won't."

"Challenge accepted." She pointed at her suitcases. "Stow those bags aboard and we'll get ready to leave."

He didn't immediately grab them. On the contrary, he crossed his arms over his impressive chest and declared, "I am not your manservant. Do it yourself."

"Me?" Her eyes widened. "You can't seriously expect a lady to carry her own bags?"

"Lady?" He snorted. "You were just stark naked on a runway."

"An unfortunate side effect of shifting."

"Shifting to chase after a car."

"Someone was shooting at us. A lady sometimes has to do dirty things to protect herself since the male on the scene didn't act."

"Are you saying it's my fault you turned into a kitty?" While his voice never changed pitch, she heard the incredulity.

"Most definitely your fault. Had you gone after the shooter like a proper man, we wouldn't be having this discussion. I really have to wonder why Gaston chose you as his second-in-command. Your security skills leave much to be desired."

"Nothing wrong with my skills." He almost growled the words.

"If you say so, sweetcheeks. You can show me those skills later so I can be the judge." She patted his face before walking past him. Hands empty of course.

"I think you forgot something."

She whirled with a gasp. "How could I be so remiss?" She smiled at him as she sauntered to the car, hips swinging, drawing his gaze.

A predator always knew how to lull its prey.

Walking past him, she leaned over the passenger side of the convertible and grabbed her purse. "Mustn't forget this," she said as she walked back toward the plane. As she passed him, she tucked the fiver she'd grabbed from her purse into the breast pocket of his dark jacket. "That's for your troubles."

Then she kept going, feeling the laser heat of his stare. A grin split her lips.

This trip is going to be so much fun. How much longer before sweetcheeks exploded?

CHAPTER FOUR

DID she seriously just tip me?

The balls on this woman were huge. He couldn't believe they didn't drag on the ground they were so massive.

Yet, as frustrating as JF found her attitude, he couldn't help a grudging admiration. Stacey acted like a princess, and the role suited her.

Despite the fact she'd recently shifted and gone after a shooter, she looked as if she'd just stepped out of a salon. Her rich red hair tumbled down over her bared shoulders. Her creamy skin required no artifice to show-case her beauty. The dress she wore accentuated her feminine attributes.

Good enough to eat.

But totally off-limits.

JF didn't get involved with shifters. Ever. Nor did he cater to them. Ordering him around as if she had a right.

It occurred to him he should ignore her command and leave her shit in the car. He wasn't some lackey she commanded at will, and yet...much as it pained him, her expectation of gallantry tugged at something in him, tugged at the old JF who used to not think twice about opening a door for a woman or carrying boxes because they were heavy. One betrayal by the fairer sex and he now couldn't be bothered to even try.

Perhaps it was time he started again. Found those old manners his mother had instilled in him.

He peeked into the trunk, saw the two large suitcases and the one much smaller one.

"Would you hurry up already, sweetcheeks? We have a flight to make."

Maybe he'd start being a gentleman, with everyone but her. Princess needed a lesson in how to treat people.

JF boarded the plane and sat down, noting Stacey coming out of the washroom at the back, her natural features enhanced by the addition of some lip-gloss and mascara.

She smiled at him, a brilliant beaming grin of satisfaction. He couldn't wait to smother it.

"Was that so hard to do, sweetcheeks?"

"Not at all. Why, one would say I barely exerted myself."

"Did you close the baggage compartment?"

"You mean the one I never opened?"

"What is that supposed to mean?" Stacey frowned and peeked out the door. "The trunk is still open on my car. Do you mean to say you didn't bring the bags?"

"Bring them yourself if you're that keen on having clothes. Given I wasn't warned about this trip, and didn't pack a thing for myself, I'd say that would make us even."

"Would it help if I said I picked up some things for

you? After all, if you're going to play the part of my brother, we should at least look like we're related."

"Brother?" The thoughts she invoked were much too carnal for someone that might be related to her. Then again, given her attitude, and her very nature, it shouldn't take long to destroy any urges he felt toward her.

"Yes, brother. I couldn't very well make you my boyfriend. I am, after all, going there as bait for the guy who's been kidnapping women."

"What are you talking about? Explain yourself, woman."

"I can't explain right now because apparently I have to move my own luggage because someone's mother didn't love him enough to teach him proper manners."

The rebuke stung, mostly because his mother had taught him better than this. But surely even his mother would understand why he acted this way after what had happened to him.

Sitting down, he refused to feel guilt. He heard a few thumps as the baggage was stowed. Another thump as the car trunk was closed.

He didn't stir at all until he heard the rev of several engines and the smash of a chain-link fence getting torn down. A most distinctive sound, as was the screech of tires.

What the fuck? Had that gunman returned? As he went to look out the door, Stacey came flying in, shoving him out of her way. "We need to go," she announced.

As JF stared out the door, several cars screamed to a halt alongside her convertible.

Whatever happened next he missed because she pulled on the portal and slammed it shut.

"That's not going to do us much good. The pilot's not here yet," he remarked. The cockpit sat empty, the lights on the dash illuminated, the engines humming softly.

"The pilot is on board, sweetcheeks."

He couldn't help but utter a horrified, "No," as she plopped herself in the pilot's chair. She began to toggle things, and the engines' quiet purring turned to a rumble as the plane lurched forward.

"You don't seriously expect me to believe you can drive this thing."

"The correct term is pilot. And you can believe it or not, up to you. I, though, plan to get us out of here."

There was still time for him to jump out while the plane picked up speed. He crouched down for a peek out the window in time to see the red sports car ignite.

"I think they just torched your ride."

"Those jerks! The dealership I borrowed it from is going to be pissed."

"Can you really fly this thing?" JF pushed into the cockpit, the tight space not meant for his bulk. Sitting in the front meant being close to the maniac woman intent on running over the men standing in the middle of the runway.

Men with guns aimed right at them.

"They're going to shoot."

"Possibly."

"What do you mean possibly?"

"I don't think they will. Haven't you ever played chicken before? Or the game where you wait to see who is going to blink first? Rest assured, sweetcheeks, it is not going to be me." She aimed the plane right at those men.

She was wrong. They didn't blink.

The muzzles of their weapons flashed as they fired, and yet, while the bullets impacted the windshield, it didn't crack.

"Gotta love quality pride construction," Stacey crowed.

At the moment, JF loved it very much, too, since it meant he didn't hear any hissing that would have indicated a breach.

Since their initial plan failed, the men aimed lower.

"Ooh, those jerks. They're shooting at the wheels." She tugged on the controls, and the plane lurched to the side then veered back, still picking up speed.

The men on the tarmac moved out of the way rather than try and stop it with their bodies. JF craned to see them running back to the pile of cars. One of the vehicles began to chase them down the runway.

"They're going to cut you off," he declared.

"No, they're not," she replied with a fierce smile. "Hold on tight."

Hold on to what? He'd already left his sanity behind, apparently.

His body flattened into his seat as the plane pulled, the front part of it leaving the ground. He swallowed hard, especially as a car at the top of the runway executed a sharp turn and aimed at them.

It began barreling at the airplane. Too late to do any damage. The little aircraft kept pulling into the air, the ascent sharp. The plane left the ground with enough altitude that they skimmed over the car.

But that wasn't why he white-knuckled the seat.

Stacey noticed and asked, "What's wrong?"

"I hate flying," he muttered through gritted teeth.

"That makes no sense. Whampyrs have wings. Your kind can fly."

"Different thing. When I'm in my whampyr shape, I'm flying, me and only me, not trusting some lunatic cat driving some oversized coffin with wings and propellers."

"Pussy."

"I am not a pussy."

"So you won't freak out if I do this?" By this she meant take her hands off the controls.

The plane didn't suddenly go into a sharp dive, but he still yelled, "Drive the fucking plane, woman!"

"Calm down, sweetcheeks. This baby isn't going to crash." His shoulders dropped a little in relief at her confident tone. "Unless they hit something vital with their bullets."

The tension came back with friends. "You are not funny."

"Depends on who you ask. My biatches think I'm awesome. My enemies on the other hand...they know I mean business."

Looking at her profile, the snub nose, the fine features, the sweet lilt of her lips, he couldn't help but scoff. "Exactly how many enemies can you really have?"

"Too many to count. I am the scourge of the rodent population. The elegant death to those who might harm the pride. A soul crusher to those that would adore me and yet not meet my high standards."

"And what are your standards?" He blamed the tension still riding him for asking. He had no interest. Who cared about this woman and what she liked in a man?

I sure as hell don't. Yet, for some reason, he listened intently to her reply.

"I like a well-groomed man, suit and tie especially. Business oriented, the white collar, pencil-pushing kind. I am partial to smooth fingers." She purred the words. "I want a gentleman, the kind who knows how to treat a lady in and out of the bedroom."

"Sounds boring."

"Only because you're obviously not the type of man I'm looking for."

"Good, because you're not my type either." Barked out at her mostly because, and surely this was wrong, he felt offended. Offended at her rejection? It was only rejection if he gave a fuck, which he didn't. Not one bit.

"What kind of woman do you like?" she asked.

"The kind that doesn't talk."

"A guy into necrophilia. I guess with your boss being a necromancer that's not too much of a stretch."

"I don't fuck the dead."

"The mute?"

"No. I meant I don't like women who yap all the time and waste the air around them."

"So, in other words, just another guy who gets in and out as quick as he can, with no finesse."

"I have plenty of finesse." Again, why did he feel a need to reply?

"Says you, sweetcheeks. I'm going to need proof of that."

Show her. Drag her out of that seat and shut her up.

No.

And not just because she was driving the plane. No getting involved with shifters. Especially not this one.

27

The very fact that she drew him was a warning sign to stay away.

The plane leveled off, and she clapped her hands. "Next stop, Caribbean destination. You may unbuckle and move around the cabin if you like."

He did like. The interior of the cockpit was too small to avoid her. Her scent. Her smile. The fact that he knew under that dress she didn't wear a single extra stitch. How easy it would be to slide his hand under the skirt of her dress and touch the pink folds she'd so brazenly displayed to him before.

I wouldn't mind a lick...

He bolted from the front into the more comfortable passenger section with its leather couch and captain-style seats. JF sat down, closed his eyes, and sighed.

"Homesick already?" she asked, following him.

"What the fuck are you doing? Get back in there and drive the plane." He jabbed a finger in the direction of the cockpit.

"Relax, sweetcheeks. I've got it on autopilot. We're fine. If anything weird crops up, something will beep. Usually."

"And if it doesn't?"

"There's a parachute around here somewhere, I'm sure."

"The right answer is nothing is going to happen."

"Then where would the fun be? Lighten up."

"I'll lighten up when people aren't trying to make me into bloody Swiss cheese. Who was that shooting at you back at the airstrip?" Because when he'd told Gaston about it, Gaston had sounded surprised at the attack.

"Good question." She shrugged. "Could be any

28

number of people, but it's most likely my ex-boyfriend. He's got a bit of a temper."

"Nice taste in guys. What happened to dating pencil-pushing pansies?"

"A mistake, I'll admit. Michael wasn't who he said he was. He told me he was into imports and exports. Except what he forgot to say was those involved drugs. I don't approve of drugs, and I hate liars. So I had him arrested and put in jail."

"You put a drug dealer you were dating in jail?" He gaped at her.

"Him and a good chunk of his crew. I hear a judge let him out early for good behavior."

"And now he's trying to kill you."

"Can you blame him? Because he chose a life of crime, he lost out on this." She referred to her curves.

Don't look.

He couldn't help himself. She was like some evil idol carved to perfection, made to force a man to lust after something he didn't want.

Lie. I want her. Want to grab her by the hair, bend her over, and do things to her that would feel so fucking good. But he wouldn't. Because bestiality was against the law.

"I need a drink," she stated. "I don't suppose you'd fetch me one."

"Not a chance, princess."

"Figures," she muttered as she headed to the back, only she didn't make it far.

Did she intentionally trip on his lap? What happened to felines having exceptional balance and grace?

Whatever the case, she fell, right on top of him.

JF caught her but not before her bottom squished onto his lap.

"Oops. How clumsy of me. I hope I didn't hurt you." She smiled at him coyly.

He recognized the game. "You can stop trying."

"Trying what?" She batted her lashes.

"To goad me. To flirt. I've been assigned to you as a guard. No more. I'm not your toy, nor am I at all interested in your charms."

"Not even a little?" She squirmed on his lap, and he quickly set her away from him.

"Behave yourself, woman."

"Why would I do that?"

"Because ladies don't throw themselves at virtual strangers."

"Lighten up, sweetcheeks."

"No. We should be discussing those men who were shooting at you and what to do in case they try again." Not thinking of how easily he could pull her close and nuzzle her mound.

"What makes you think they were shooting at me?"

"You just told me it was your ex-convict ex-boyfriend."

"No, I said it was a possibility. But that doesn't mean it was him. After all, Michael really did enjoy himself with me. Why would he kill me when he could kidnap me and make me his sex slave?"

"You'd seriously go back to a drug dealer?"

"Of course not, but it would be romantic if he tried. As to shooting, who's to say those guys weren't after you? You are, after all, working for a necromancer. Which is seriously cool. Do you have an idea how many jealous biatches there are in the pride? Reba scored huge when she snared Gaston. Who doesn't want a boyfriend who could raise the undead?"

"They weren't shooting at me," he growled. Surely not jealous that Stacey showed such admiration for Gaston. She'd obviously never seen the man's taste in music.

"How can you be sure?" she asked.

"For one thing, no one knew I would be at the airstrip."

"And what makes you think anyone knew I was? We lions are stealthy creatures."

"You are not stealthy. People for miles around probably see you coming in that little red sports car."

"You have a point. The attention that baby draws is totally worth the chunk off my paycheck."

"It blew up."

"No, it sacrificed itself that I might get a newer model courtesy of my insurance company. She smiled quite happily.

"Perhaps the shooters are related to whatever business you've got planned in the Caribbean."

"That would be exciting if they were related."

Much as he wanted to show disinterest, even JF knew when he was taking stubbornness too far. "What exactly are you going to this island for?"

"Ever watch *The X-Files*?"

"Isn't that a fictional show with aliens?"

"Yes. About a duo of investigators, Mulder and Scully, hunting for clues to solve supernatural mysteries."

"Did this Mulder solve crimes with the help of his cat?"

She gaped. "I thought you saw this show."

"No."

"There is no cat. I'm Scully in this scenario, the brains of the operation, and you're Mulder, off doing his own thing. In this case, just stay out of my way so you don't cramp my style."

"Because God forbid anyone introduce rationality and a cautious approach to a situation."

"See, already you're trying to bring a level of boring to this. You're just along for the ride because Arik said I couldn't go alone. Some sort of concern I'd disappear like the other broads did."

"What other broads?"

"I don't know about all of them. But Shania was apparently kidnapped by a lion-headed man."

He blinked at her. "Did you drug me?" Because surely he'd misunderstood.

"Why would you think I drugged you? Unless"—her expression brightened—"my very attractive pheromones are affecting you."

"They're not. But something must be in the air making me hear things because I could have sworn you said a woman was kidnapped by a lion-headed man." Which made no sense.

"You heard me right. I'm supposed to find out what the deal is with the liotaur. Which is kind of like a minotaur but with a lion's head."

JF pressed his lips together rather than say anything about the made-up name. What the fuck had Gaston sent him into?

And why did a part of him look forward to the adventure—with her?

CHAPTER FIVE

THE MAN DIDN'T KNOW how to smile. Stacey was convinced of it, and the more she explained about the liotaur, the deeper the frown on his face got. So deep she wondered if it was a permanent affliction.

"So, in summary, sweetcheeks, my role is to dig up dirt and dangle myself as bait, while you, acting as my dopey older brother, stay out of the way."

"I'm pretty sure I'm supposed to keep you from coming to harm."

"You, act chivalrous?" She smiled. "I wouldn't want you to hurt yourself." She patted his cheek. "But tell you what, if you really want to give chivalry a shot, then feel free to carry my bags and fetch me drinks."

"I'm here as your bodyguard, not your personal butler."

"I don't require a guard. I am perfectly capable of taking care of myself, not to mention I don't need you messing things up. How am I supposed to seem abductable if you're always around scowling?"

"I don't scowl."

"You don't smile either."

"How's this?" He showed a lot of teeth.

She recoiled. "Don't do that. You'll give people nightmares."

"Funny, I would have said the same of you. When the pride comes around, it's batten down the hatches and hide your fragile belongings."

"Because we know how to have a good time. You should take lessons."

"From who? You?" He snickered. "What makes you think you're better than me?"

Did he really need an answer? "I'm a lion, so of course I'm better than you. I'm better than just about anyone other than another lion." She rolled her eyes in a duh fashion.

"Felines have got to be the most exasperating animals to deal with," he mumbled.

"Thank you. It's on account we're so regal and intelligent."

"More like pea-brained and oblivious."

"No wonder you're single, sweetcheeks. That is not how you charm a lady."

"I'm sorry, was there a lady around here?" He looked around, and she had to laugh.

"Naughty, naughty. You can pretend, but I have a hunch you like what you see."

"I'd get your hunches checked out by a pro because I am going to state, right now, I have no interest in getting a house cat."

"Not even if I told you I had a fetish for licking skin?"

"Not even if you cooked and cleaned."

Her nose wrinkled. "Ugh. Why would I do that? You see these hands?" She held up her perfectly manicured fingers. "These hands aren't made for hot soapy water or gross sponges."

"Then what are you good for?"

"Many things."

"Such as? What's your job?"

"Event coordinator for the pride."

He snorted. "So you're a party girl. What a surprise."

"I'll have you know my position with the pride is complicated. It's not easy getting large gatherings to go off without a hitch."

"You mean you can't just throw down a side of beef and ring a bell?"

Her lips twitched. "Depends on the occasion."

"So, if this case is so serious, why send you? Don't they have a security team better equipped for this?"

"Arik wants to keep this quiet until he knows what's going on. He's most perturbed that people have been keeping it a secret from him. This investigation is being done on the down-low. Which is where I come in. My job as event coordinator looking to put together a wedding is going to give me access at the resort to things we might not see as guests."

"Seems awfully complicated. A woman is missing. Why not just hunt the fellow down and fetch her back?"

"Because no one has been able to find a trace. A rainfall wiped the place clean. Not a single scent has been located."

"Bet you I could find one. Give me a day."

"You want to go looking? Go ahead. It will at least keep you out of my path."

"You're really arrogant, you know."

"And you're not?" she said with a teasing smile.

"Not my fault I'm superior to you."

"If I didn't know better, I'd say you were a lion."

He shuddered. "Now that's just being mean."

"You'll take offense at that, and yet you're the one who's been insulting me at every turn."

"I don't want to be here."

"So you keep saying and yet..." She crouched down in front of him, placed her hands on his taut thighs, and smiled. "I can tell when a man is interested in me."

His gaze met hers, the spark within a sign. "I'd have to be dead to not want to fuck you. But I don't need to like you to do that. A pussy is a pussy."

"But we're not all made the same."

"Turn off the lights and there's no difference."

"You'd know it was me. I guarantee it, sweetcheeks."

"Doubtful. Women are all the same." He didn't say it as if it were a positive thing.

She'd have to change his mind. "Another challenge. What fun."

"What are you talking about?"

"I'm talking about the fact you keep tossing down the gauntlet. Well, guess what, sweetcheeks, I am picking that gauntlet up. By the end of this trip, not only will we be lovers, you'll like me. A lot." Heck, if Mr. Cool and Arrogant played his cards right, she might even extend their fling past their sojourn on the island.

"I thought I wasn't your type." He held up his hands. "Callused fingers."

"There's manicures for that."

"I don't want to be your boyfriend."

"I never said your lover status would be permanent. I doubt you'll keep me entertained for long, which will suck for you when I move on." She stood and walked toward the cockpit.

"Or, maybe, princess, you'll be the one asking me to stay, and I'll be the one leaving you high and dry."

Her, fall for a man who thought she should carry her own luggage? Never.

"Strap in, sweetcheeks, we're starting our descent." And the game to see who would win started now.

CHAPTER SIX

DESPITE ALL JF'S MISGIVINGS, they landed
without mishap, the plane taxiing with barely a bump as
it hit the tarmac, slowing to a stop as it reached the proper
spot by the terminal.

Kind of disappointing really. He'd entertained a
fantasy where he had to jump from the plane, soar on his
big wings, and then made her beg to be saved.

But the flying tin can landed without mishap, if one
ignored the state of his mind after spending a few hours
with the feline.

JF couldn't wait to set foot on solid ground. If only
he could escape the woman responsible for his presence
on a tropical island. While her mission on the island
might have merit, he could just imagine the disaster
she'd make of the execution. What was the lion king
thinking?

Surely no one thought this flighty princess could
really make a difference?

The door to the craft opened, and the freshness of the

air, hinting of airplane exhaust and redolent jungle blooms, tickled his nose.

So many smells. Things to hunt.

The beast within looked forward to a change in diet. He, on the other hand, could already tell he'd miss the cool crisp weather of fall approaching back home.

Heat, the moist kind that dampened the skin, filled the cabin, curling the ends of his hair. His naturally cooler body temperature kept him from sweating, but he'd probably have to ditch his coat. Which sucked. JF preferred to dress in layers.

Emerging into the sunlight, he provided a large target at the top of the stairs, a scowling target, as someone jabbed a sharp nail into his spine.

"Are you going to move that big butt of yours or stand there hogging the stairs all day?" Stacey asked, pushing at him. As if she could move him.

"Don't test me, woman."

"Afraid you'll fail? What if I promised to make it multiple choice?"

Why did she take everything he said and spin it? It made a man want to duct tape her mouth—or shove something in it.

I have something just the right size...

He went down the steps and noted a pair of people walking in from the terminal, both strangers dressed in crisp white linen. Shorts for the guy and a tennis skirt for the female. They could have been siblings with their matching golden locks.

Not even on the ground two minutes and he'd wager already he'd found some lions. And they said rabbits multiplied all over the place. At least rabbit tasted delicious, especially when fresh. Speaking of which, he'd have to find a source for feeding.

How about eating Princess?

Tempting, but gnawing on her probably wouldn't go over well. Gaston had a thing about his minions eating humans and shifters. Something about only cannibals ate sentient beings. Personally, JF thought his boss gave the shifters too much credit. Teaching them to talk didn't make them evolved.

As to those who might question his snobbery? The only thing above a whampyr was the necromancer who helped make them. And even then...whampyrs were not to be trifled with.

"You must be Stacey." The man with short blond hair wearing thigh-length white shorts and a pink shirt approached with his hand outstretched and a smile on his face. A smile that faltered, as JF kept frowning.

"Who are you?" JF barked as he scanned the stranger for a weapon.

"Um, I'm Maurice. I'm from Club Lyon. I am here to provide transportation and get you settled into the resort."

"Where's your identification?" Not that JF needed more than a sniff. The cloying scent of lion filled his nostrils. For a young cub, the boy exuded a strong aroma.

"Ignore my brother. Flying makes him grumpy." Stacey pushed past him. "Hi, I'm Stacey. Delighted to meet you." Balancing the package she'd brought from the plane, she shook the man's hands, and JF did his best to not growl.

The sight of her touching the other man ignited something primitive in him that he couldn't explain. He didn't sense any danger. On the contrary, the young man appeared nervous, which, in turn, made him seem weak.

Yet, knowing he could probably knock him out with a single punch didn't stop JF's scowl. It did, however, cause Maurice to pull his hand free and take a step back.

"Now look at what you've done," Stacey exclaimed before pouting. "You're being grumpy again."

"It was a long flight. He's probably thirsty and hungry," the woman by Maurice's side offered with a shy smile in his direction.

"And who are you?" Stacey asked, her tone sour, a princess interrupted.

"I'm Jan. I'm also with guest resources. Let me know about anything you need to make your stay more memorable," she said softly, the words aimed directly at him.

A wasted effort. She smelled almost as strongly as Maurice did of feline. He already had his hands full enough with Stacey, thank you very much. No need for him to attract another stray.

Stacey stepped in front of him, forcing Jan to meet her gaze. "My very own concierge. How wonderful. And yet you appeared with no drink?"

Jan's lips tightened. "Sorry. We have water bottles in the Jeep."

"Water?" Stacey's nose wrinkled. "I thought this was paradise."

"As soon as we reach the resort, we can find something more palatable for you."

Switching gears, Stacey turned from Jan to Maurice and gushed. "I can't wait to hear all about the resort. Arik's told me how wonderful it is. Melly doesn't know we're planning a surprise destination wedding for her." As Stacey blathered, JF fought to not roll his eyes.

What a load of crap. Why all the acting? Why not just tell people why they were really here?

You have people missing. Tell us everything you know. Or else...

After years of living in subterfuge, he was tired of it. Tired of hiding. However, this wasn't his mission. He was just along as muscle. Which was fine with him. He had no interest in getting involved in pride problems. Let the cats sort it out themselves.

"Oh, brother, be a dear and grab our bags while I use the ladies room and freshen up." Stacey didn't give him time to reply, as she turned and sauntered off, arm in arm with Jan toward the terminal.

"I am not your bloody servant," he muttered, only to realize Maurice remained behind.

"Women never give a guy any respect," said the young man with a wan smile. "A word of advice. If you like your sister at all, you should get her away from here."

"Why?" JF asked, trying for nonchalance instead of surprise. Not even on the ground five minutes and strange shit was happening.

"It's not safe right now on the island."

Heading for the cargo area of the plane, JF was able to sound casual as he asked, "What's going on? Having problems with that Zika virus we've been hearing about?"

"No, not a virus. What I'm talking about is something more dangerous, and only to someone like your sister."

"Annoying, self-absorbed, and demanding?" He pulled out the suitcases and tried not to grunt at their weight. No wonder she didn't want to lug them around. Had she packed cement in them?

"Women have been disappearing."

"Women as in more than one?" he asked casually as he lugged the two biggest bags to the golf cart parked nearby. Maurice managed to strong-arm the smaller bag on top of them.

"Three in the last few months have disappeared."

Three. Stacey had mentioned the one from the resort and a history of others in the past. Was someone covering up their disappearances?

"Are they dead?"

"Not that we know of."

"Then why assume they've been taken? They could have gone native." Not unusual by any means. Beautiful woman comes to paradise, meets a native of the area. A surfing instructor, yoga coach, salsa dancer. They're swept off their feet and decide to start a new life instead of returning to their old one.

"They didn't go native. They were kidnapped."

"Appalling." The right thing to say, even if he didn't particularly care. "Do the police have any leads?"

"The police aren't investigating. They think the girls just wandered off."

"But you don't believe that. Why?"

Maurice kept his head ducked as he went around to the far side of the cart. "It's not safe here. If you love your sister at all, you'll take her and run before she disappears too."

JF couldn't help himself. He leaned close to the little guy and said, "Actually, we're not close. Different mothers. I don't even like her that much. She's a brat. And it sure would solve some inheritance problems if she were to disappear. Any tips on making her more attractive to whoever is doing it?"

The gaping mouth and wide eyes almost made JF chuckle.

Almost.

Until he heard the scream.

CHAPTER SEVEN

STACEY COULDN'T STOP SHRIEKING. It was terrifying. Utterly terrifying. Which was why when Jean Francois banged on the bathroom stall door, slamming the flimsy portal open, she leaped from her spot atop the toilet into his arms.

Built of solid stone, the man didn't even stagger, nor did he drop her. Good thing because that would have put her too close to the *thing* sitting at the foot of the toilet.

"What the fuck is going on?" he yelled.

She got the impression he yelled a lot. It didn't really bother her. Especially since he had a nice deep rumble.

"Protect me from that monster. Kill it!" Stacey pointed at the arachnid that had dared crawl into her stall while she sent a few texts back home. She'd opted for a visit to the bathroom where she could get a Wi-Fi signal and some privacy. What she'd not counted on was being interrupted. It was only by chance she noted the disgusting hairy thing heading for her open-toed sandals.

"You're screaming as if you're being murdered because of a fucking spider?"

Arms wrapped around his neck, legs around his torso, she was pressed too tight to see his face, but she could hear his incredulity.

"It's not just any spider. It's a big spider. With hair." So much hair, sob. "And legs." Just remembering all those legs moving sent a shudder through her.

Squish.

"There, are you happy now?"

Gag. "No. I heard that." She gagged a bit more. "Ugh. I can't believe you stepped on it." More heaving. "It's probably all over your shoe."

"It is. You're right; it was big. And very squishy. Want to see?"

When he began to crouch, she sprang away from him, away from the stall and the scene of the disgusting spider carnage.

"I hate you," she declared as she marched out of the bathroom. She glared at her blonde guide, who pretended innocence, but Stacey saw right through the girl. There was something sly about her. Something Stacey didn't like. Especially how Jan eyeballed her fake brother when he exited the bathroom.

"Thank you for taking care of your sister," Jan simpered. "I would have done something, but she wouldn't let me in."

Well duh. "Opening the door would have required stepping onto the floor." Which would then have given the bloodthirsty arachnid a chance to attack.

Jean Francois snorted. "If you're done being a big baby, then our stuff is probably out front by now."

"Arachnophobia is a documented medical condition."

"Also known as being a pussy," he retorted. "It was a spider. About as dangerous as a fly."

"I'll have you know spiders kill people every year with their bite. And flies are known disease carriers."

"Would you like some cheese to go with your whine, princess pussy?"

"See if I save you when you scream because your life is in danger," Stacey grumbled.

"You won't have to because, unlike you, *sis*," he said in a mocking tone, "I'm not afraid of anything."

"We'll see about that," she murmured as she walked past him. Even the biggest, boldest of men feared something. Once she discovered his weakness, she'd exploit it, just like she used Joan's love of jalapeno cheese dip against her whenever Stacey wanted to borrow that red dress of hers. Joan was spice intolerant but couldn't resist the lure of nachos and cheese sauce. Which then bloated her, which meant Stacey could scoop up that hot red number and paint the town.

If Joan were smart, she'd just give in and gift the damned dress to Stacey. Then again, part of the reason she enjoyed wearing it so much was the challenge in getting it in the first place.

Their ride to the resort wasn't in a car but an open-top Jeep with four spots. Maurice, of course, took the wheel, but instead of Jan sitting beside him, she slid into the back and patted the bench beside her. "We should give your sister the front. The windshield will block some of the wind from messing up her hair."

Then Jan tittered.

Stacey hated tittering. Especially at her expense. Did

this little kitten seriously think to challenge her? Playing up to Jean Francois as if she had a right?

He's mine. Which in turn made her frown. He was here as a cover and shield only. Not as potential boyfriend material, no matter how sexy she found him. For one thing, he wasn't a big-time business man. Or a lion.

She could handle maybe a bear, or a wolf. Even another necromancer fellow would have the right kind of genes and prestige to make her momma happy. But a simple assistant to a bar owner? One that wasn't even really a shifter or a vampire?

I can do better than that. She deserved better than Mr. Dour Face in the back.

Determined to ignore him, she slid in the front and not once looked back at him—or the little tart surely pressing herself against him.

Stacey made conversation with Maurice, who answered all her questions about the island.

It wasn't a very large island, less than a hundred square miles with a chunk of it left undeveloped.

"You see that over there?" Maurice took a hand off the wheel to point at a lush green mountain. "That's a volcano. It's dormant now, has been for ages, but the natives in the area hold it sacred, which means the mountain itself and the area around it is protected."

"How many people on the island?"

Apparently, that number depended on the resorts themselves. If counting only the locals, then only a few thousand residents. But the resorts themselves swelled that number, especially in peak seasons.

Stacey could see why. They were literally in

paradise. Warm weather, lush foliage, and a land bursting with life.

There were only a few vehicles on the road, most of them short buses and vans, emblazoned with the names of resorts. Of houses and other amenities, they saw little, the road from the airport mostly traveling through chunks of jungle, intersected only by other roads, usually bordered by a sign with the name of the business. Club Paradise. Beach Club. Club Springs.

A lack of originality existed with the names, but they all promised one thing in common. A spectacular vacation.

But I'm not here to relax and unwind. She was here to find out what had happened to Shania. Maybe hook up with the liotaur and make her biatches jealous.

I wonder if Jean Francois gets jealous.

A cold and lacking in humor man, he probably didn't have enough passion in him to care.

Heck, did the man even enjoy sex?

She thought she'd felt an erection when she plopped herself on his lap, but she didn't stay on it long enough to be sure.

I should totally try again. A decision that made no sense. She didn't like the guy. At all. However, she had to know. *Does he find me attractive?*

Maurice certainly did. The poor boy couldn't look at her without blushing. So cute. Whereas Jean Francois couldn't stop scowling. Even cuter.

The gates leading into the resort were bordered by towering golden lions. The arch overhead a golden fili-gree with the name Club Lyon's Resort etched within the curlicues and fancy scrollwork. Pretty, but even the tall fence wouldn't stop someone determined to get in.

Beyond the gates lay paradise. Lush trees, the green of their leaves vivid, bordered the paved drive leading into the property. Bright blooms popped with color and exuded lovely scents, the perfume tickling her nose. She closed her eyes in pleasure as she inhaled deeply. *Smells good enough to roll in.* Because, yes, lions did so love to roll in foliage.

With her eyes still shut, she inhaled some more, this time looking past the obvious scents to filter those beneath. The exhaust from the Jeep. A touch of acrid smoke. A hint of salt in the air. The ocean was nearby. She couldn't wait to dip her toes in the warm water. After dark. Her pale skin couldn't handle the midday sun.

The Jeep pulled to a stop in front of a large building made of bleached coral. Unique and very pretty.

Maurice saw her looking. "The entire resort is built from natural resources found on the island."

"I don't know if I'd call harvesting coral to build things natural," Jean Francois stated as he jumped out the back of the Jeep. He then offered a hand to Jan, who took it with a smile.

No one helped Stacey out of the Jeep.

Maurice shook his head. "All of the materials were recycled, not harvested or cut down. The jungles have plenty of fallen trees or those in need of trimming to keep them from getting knocked over in storms. Just like the coral goes through cycles where older parts die and break off. We even use the parts that wash up on shore."

"Is that lava rock?" Stacey asked, pointing to the

darker stone mixed into the walls. "I thought I read the volcano was on protected government land."

"It is, but over the years the islanders have uncovered stashes of it outside that zone. And then, of course, there's the stuff found on the beach."

In reality, Stacey didn't truly care where the resort got its supplies. She asked because the more she knew, the more likely something would pop out at her. Joan might disparage Stacey's job as an event planner; however, the one thing she didn't understand was Stacey's ability to read situations and people. Stacey had to be good in order to avoid bridezilla situations.

Once they reached the interior of the building, the check-in process was much like other resorts. A thick silicone band was placed around her wrist, the ends sealed to prevent removal. Its presence proved her guest status with the resort.

She held it up with a smile. "Free drinks."

"Drinks. Food. Towels. Anything you need. Plus it acts as your key." Maurice showed them. "Place your wrist in front of your door, and the sensor within will allow you entry."

Fascinating technology. In the lion's pride condominium, all the various apartments had hand print scanners, but for a hotel that might prove a little excessive.

"Do all the employees have to wear one?" she asked, pointing to Maurice's wrist. Unlike her golden band, his was a deep red.

"Everyone on the property has one, even delivery people and maintenance crew. It helps us to identify who belongs."

It made her wonder if the liotaur caught on tape had

worn one as well. She thought over what she'd seen but couldn't recall. As they walked to their golf cart that held their bags, she fired off a quick text to Melly.

"Would you put that thing away?" Jean Francois grumbled. "I'm sure your Facebook status can wait a few more minutes."

"Not my fault I have friends who are interested in what I do."

"Maybe you should have brought one of your friends with you."

Because being a brat was second nature, she planted her hands on her hips and sassed back, "I'm going to tell Dad you're being mean to me again. I told him this trip wouldn't help us to bond."

His lip twitched. Just a single little muscle. But she saw it.

"Dad should have worn a condom," was his retort.

"And here I thought you were going to say my mom should have swallowed."

Poor Maurice choked, and this time, definite lip twitch on Jean Francois's face.

I will crack you yet!

The golf cart they piled into—minus Jan, who they'd left behind at registration—wound around the meandering paths crisscrossing the resort. As they flew through them, Maurice pointed out spots of interest.

"Tennis courts are at the top end of the resort, along with archery and lawn bowling. The spa is down on the eastern edge of the beach and offers indoor and outdoor options for treatment. There is yoga on the beach at dawn, as well as various other physical classes throughout the day. There is a boathouse on the western edge of the main beach offering boats, paddleboards, and kayaks to those looking for a water adventure."

As he rattled off a litany of activities, all of them involving strenuous work and sweat, from her spot in the back, Stacey instead watched her companion's granite profile.

The man rarely smiled and didn't seem at all comfortable in a tropical location. He'd yet to strip off any of his clothes. Pity. She wondered what he hid under those layers.

As it was, he looked completely and utterly out of place. Given his constant scowl, she'd have to ditch him if her attempt to bait the liotaur would work. No way would anyone try to kidnap her if her *brother* stuck too close by.

Given his intense dislike of her—which was surely feigned because hello, *I am awesome*—it probably wouldn't be hard to convince him to go in one direction while she went in another. The one that would lead her to the mystery shapeshifter.

The cart stopped in front of a pink-pastel-colored three-story building. There were two doors per level and numerous windows.

"This is the Bella building. You've been given the top floor, which has the best view."

"How many other people staying in the building?" And to cover her curiosity she added, "I'm a bit of a night kitty. I'd hate to keep any guests awake."

"Noise won't be an issue. The middle level is undergoing repair."

"And what about the bottom one?" She eyed the pulled curtains with interest.

"It's empty."

"He's lying," Jean Francois said, and Maurice visibly started.

"I am not."

"Tell her." Her companion didn't have to add "or else." The implication came through loud and clear.

Maurice sighed. "I'm not supposed to talk about it. But apparently the client who was staying in that room"—he pointed to the door ahead of them—"seems to have wandered off."

"Wandered off?" Stacey asked. "As in of her own volition? Or did someone coerce her?"

At the pointed query, Maurice squirmed. "I'm sure she's fine wherever she is. The island has a very low rate of incidents, and those are rarely violent."

"I find that hard to believe. In general, lions and other shifters are a violent bunch."

Maurice appeared startled by Jean Francois's statement.

Taking pity on him, Stacey said, "You don't have to hide what we are around my brother. While he might not be a fantabulous shifter like us, he does know about them and will keep our secret."

"I hope he can because the island natives are human."

"All of them?" she asked.

He nodded.

"But you're not."

"I'm not from here originally. Any shifters you meet working for the resort have been brought in from elsewhere."

"What's the human-to-shifter ratio on the island,

would you say?" At his sharp look, she shrugged. "Just curious. I'm planning a wedding for a friend."

"I thought you were here to bond with your brother."

"Killing two birds with one pounce," she said with a wink.

"We'd probably be closer if she wasn't working all the time," Jean Francois stated. "Why don't you show us to our rooms? Maybe then she'll try and relax."

"If you'll follow me." Maurice led them up the stairs to the top floor. A wide balcony ran the length of the building.

Maurice pointed to the door. "If you'll flash your wrist here." She waved it over the black matte square, and with a click, the door unlocked. "You have fifteen seconds to open the door before the lock engages again."

Swinging the door open, Maurice swept an arm indicating they should go in first.

Stacey stepped in, immediately noting the high ceilings and ceramic tile floors, which would help keep the room cool, along with the air conditioning unit blowing full tilt with a noisy whir. The room boasted a giant four-poster bed strung with netting, a two-seater couch and low table, plus a dresser with a television atop it. Everything looked new.

Stacey tossed her purse onto the floral bedspread before kicking off her shoes to take a peek in the bathroom. Huge and completely finished in white and an aquamarine tile, including the shower that was enclosed in glass. A soaker tub also shared the space, strategically placed in front of the window with a view of the jungle.

"This will do," she announced.

"The other room is identical," Maurice noted. "The

adjoining door between them also works with the wrist band, although you can deadbolt it should you, um, require, um, extra privacy."

While she didn't look at him, Stacey could imagine his red cheeks.

It was Arik's idea for Stacey and Jean Francois to have connecting rooms. For some reason, he thought that would keep her out of trouble.

Has he met me at all?

Only as Maurice finished their interior tour, pointing out the safe in the closet, the various toiletries available at no extra cost, plus the hidden mini bar, did she ask, "You must know the island pretty well by now. Tell me, where does a lioness go if she wants to tan au naturel?"

"Already looking for ways to shed your clothes?" Her spoilsport snorted. "Why am I not surprised?"

Maurice, though, understood her question. "The resort itself, as mentioned, is staffed by a mixture of local humans and shifters who've been brought in. We couldn't make it entirely lions or the local government might have noticed something amiss and protested. As such, we don't have any safe zones on the grounds themselves, but..." Maurice headed to the wide sliding glass doors that led to the balcony. "Over to the east, there is that dormant volcano I told you about with land that is considered protected space. While people can roam, they are not to damage the jungle or climb the volcano itself. It's too dangerous. That rule obviously doesn't extend to any local wildlife. The inside of the volcano is an especially good spot for sun bathing. And if you roar, it echoes."

"Awesome." Because no lion worth its fur would

want to miss a chance to lie in the tropical sun wearing their feline skin.

"Do you have any questions, sir?" Maurice asked Francois.

"Where's the nearest bar?"

Stacey clapped her hands. "An excellent idea, brother dear. Let us get elegantly wasted."

With that, she shooed Maurice out then turned on JF. "Have a drink for me."

"What are you planning?" he asked, his arms folded, looking absolutely forbidding.

And sexy.

"You heard what Maurice said. The missing Shania was staying on the first floor."

"Not even here an hour and you're planning to break and enter, aren't you?"

"Break?" She smiled. "Professionals don't have to smash their way in. Not when they have specials apps." She held up her phone.

"Are you saying you have a lock-picking app on your device?"

"I've got something better. A biatch who knows her coding shit." She checked her messages and smiled. "And did I mention Melly hacks in her spare time too?"

She opened the app specially installed on her phone before she left. When prompted, she held her bracelet against it until she heard a beep. Then she reached for his arm. Her fingers made contact with his skin, and a jolt went through her. Static electricity times a zillion and it all coalesced into one place on her body.

Startled, her eyes met his, and she noticed them glowing. Red.

Kind of evil.

Pretty cool.

And all for me.

Her lips curved. "Hold your band here for a second," she said, pressing his wrist against her phone until it beeped. "You can now go anywhere you want."

"Will this leave any traces in their system?"

"Are you calling Melly sloppy?" She snorted. "Of course it won't. We now have something better than a master key to anything we want in this place. We have a ghost key, which means we can get in and out without anyone knowing."

"You do realize if you can do this so easily, so can others."

"Exactly, which is why we can't believe anything they or their computers tell us. So keep that in mind when you're having that drink."

"Oh, I'm not leaving you alone, princess."

"Why, sweetcheeks, is this your way of saying you want to come with me to check out Shania's room?"

"It's my way of ensuring you don't get into trouble."

She snickered. "Yeah, just so you're forewarned, having you nearby won't stop that from happening."

"What excuse do we use if we're caught?"

"Excuse?" She scoffed. "Excuses are for pussies. I boldly go wherever I want. If I get caught, I flash some boobs."

He looked down at his chest. "Some of us don't have that advantage."

"I don't know about that, sweetcheeks. An impressive set of abs sometimes works just as well."

"So, if caught, whore myself. Is what you're saying?"

"I prefer the term using what nature blessed me with."

"Or you could just stay out of trouble in the first place."

That remark earned him a wet raspberry. "Listen, sweetcheeks, if you're too chicken to come with me, then hit the bar or stay in our rooms. I don't really care what you do." Unless he planned to jerk off. Then she might want to watch. "I'm going." Out she went, closing the door behind her since he didn't seem inclined to follow.

She skipped down the stairs, glad in one respect she didn't have to deal with him, annoyed in another because she'd not taken him for a rule-following coward. The man possessed the kind of self-assurance seen in someone who led. On a positive note, his lack of adventure detracted from his overall good looks.

Upon reaching the bottom level, a quick peek around showed no one watching, so she waved her wrist in front of the door and, when it clicked, opened it.

As she went to step in, a hand slapped over her mouth and she was dragged into the room, and the door slammed shut behind her.

CHAPTER EIGHT

"FUCKING HELL!" he yelled as Stacey's elbow jabbed him in the stomach, her foot slammed down on his instep, and her head slammed back, jarring against his chin.

His grip loosened enough that she broke free and whirled, spotting him. She didn't stop, though. Her foot slammed into his ankle, and aided by a firm shove, she sent him toppling to the floor. Then pounced him.

Surprise at her skills kept him on the ground—that and the fact that she sat atop him, eyes sparking, tits heaving, and the core of her pressed firmly against him.

His body noticed.

She also noticed, which meant he was treated to a slow, unfolding grin.

"Well hello there, sweetcheeks." She squirmed atop him, and even as his body reacted, his cock hardening to the point of throbbing, he scowled.

"What did you do that for?"

"Asks the man who thought he would manhandle me."

"I was proving a point that you weren't paying attention."

"Oh please, sweetcheeks, I'm not new at the game of cat and mouse. I knew you were there."

"Then why did you let me grab you?"

"I was hoping you were about to throw me against a wall and ravish me."

"Like fuck," he snapped. Although it had crossed his mind.

"We could fuck." She wiggled atop him some more, subjecting him to a cruel form of torture. "Just say please."

"Bite me."

"Where?" said with a taunting smile.

Below the belt, duh. A retort he kept to himself. "Who taught you to fight dirty like that?" Because he'd certainly not expected it from her. And yet he should have. He'd seen some of the lionesses in battle before. But Stacey seemed different from them. Softer, more feminine. Obviously he should have paid more attention to the red hair.

"All of the pride cubs learn how to protect ourselves from birth. Really, sweetcheeks, you should have known better."

"Just testing your skills, princess."

Let's test her oral skills. He couldn't blame the dark beast inside for that suggestion.

"How did you get in here before me?" she asked. "You didn't pass me on the stairs."

"I jumped from the balcony"—employing a quick shift back and forth that cleared him of all scent—"and let myself in through the back."

61

"Naughty man. You decided to surprise me. How adorable."

"I was trying to teach you to be more cautious."

"And instead, I taught you not to mess with me." She leaned forward, close enough that her breath washed over his face, strawberry scented like her lip-gloss. "Since I won this skirmish, do I get a prize?"

He couldn't have said why he did it. But next thing he knew, his hand clapped her on the ass, and as her eyes widened, he said, "There's your prize."

"A single spank. Seems rather cheap, if you ask me."

"Would you prefer I put you over my lap and paddle your ass?" He could see his mistake the moment the words left his mouth. Especially since her smile widened into blinding territory.

"Yes, as a matter of fact. I'd enjoy that."

"Too bad it won't happen." He rolled them suddenly, putting her on the floor so that he could leap to his feet.

He couldn't have said if it was man or beast that mournfully howled in his mind, *No!*

For a moment, she lay there, too beautiful for words, much too tempting. Even the reminder of her insanity and her feline genes couldn't stop his desire.

She wanted it. Wanted him. She'd made that rather clear. He wanted her. Wanted to grab her by that fiery red hair and thrust into her from behind.

But JF hardened himself rather than give in to his baser instincts. He'd let lust rule his head once, and it almost cost him his life. He wouldn't make that same mistake again.

Turning away from her, he took stock of the room they'd entered. The layout was identical to those upstairs with a few minor differences, namely the mess all over the place.

"Did they toss her room looking for clues?" he asked as he stepped over and around the various articles of clothing littering the floor.

"Doubtful. I think what you're seeing is a genuine slob." She pointed to the puddle of fabric beside the bed. "This is what it looks like when someone comes in a little wasted from a night of partying and manages to strip and fall into bed." She turned her finger to the suitcase, clothes overflowing its edges, the colors inside a jumbled mess. "And that is her scrounging for the perfect outfit."

"Wouldn't it make more sense to hang them?" The wrinkles alone made him shudder.

"Slobs don't care or have time to do such a thing as fold or hang them in a closet."

"You speak as if from experience."

"If you're asking if I'm a slob, then no. I love my clothes too much for that. But I am well acquainted with a few of them in the pride, which is why I feel no guilt whatsoever when I rescue certain items of clothing from them."

"You steal clothes."

"I prefer the term borrow, sometimes permanently. But only things that truly need rescuing."

"Still stealing."

"If it makes you feel better, I probably won't touch your things. But you're more than welcome to borrow mine."

Looking down at himself, then her, he said slowly, "You do realize that even if I were inclined to wear them, they wouldn't fit."

"I know, but don't you think it was generous of me to offer?"

The way her mind worked was obviously on a much different level than the rest of the world. He blamed her pea-sized cat brain.

Moving away from Stacey, JF checked into the bathroom, the countertop by the sink littered with bottles and compacts of color.

"She obviously didn't go willingly," Stacey observed. "A girl who likes her makeup would never take off without at least taking her mascara."

"Natural beauty needs no adornment."

"Nothing wrong with a little enhancement."

Any more enhancement and he might forget common sense.

Emerging back into the room proper, he took a moment to breathe in and out. Sifting scents, a few stood out.

"I smell Maurice and Jan," he intoned aloud, their flavor familiar even though they'd only met once.

"And I'll bet that banana scent is the girl." She held up a bottle of lotion with the yellow fruit on the label. "Then there are two other scents."

"A human with body odor." Who should invest in deodorant.

"And someone else. Someone that smells of lion but isn't quite right." Her nose wrinkled.

"Could be her assailant visited her room before abducting her?"

"Maybe." She drifted over to the sliding glass door, the one he'd easily popped open, the latch not hard to force. She dropped to her haunches and ran her fingers along the sliding track. She plucked free a hair. A golden strand. Holding it up, she peered at it.

"Could belong to anyone," JF stated, coming to stand close to her.

"True. But the very fact there is so much trace evidence around is bothersome. I mean I get that management or the cops might think the girl went off on her own. However, any idiot with half a brain could see she didn't take anything with her. Including her purse." The large satchel sat on the nightstand, and she went over to glance inside.

The pink case caught her eye. She pulled out a phone and pressed the power button. "It's dead."

"You probably shouldn't have touched it. Give it to me. I'll wipe your prints."

"I'm keeping it."

"I'm pretty sure you don't need to steal that girl's phone. You have one already."

She shot him an evil glare. "I am not stealing it. Mine is much better than this seventh-generation thing. I'm collecting it as evidence. Maybe we'll find something on it that will give us an idea of her plans."

"Assuming you can crack the passcode."

"Never fear, sweetcheeks, I can crack anything if I set my mind to it."

And more ominously, why could he have sworn he heard, *including you.*

WITH THE ROOM not offering up any evidence other than reinforcing the idea of foul play, they returned to their quarters—separately, with him first wiping down all the things they'd touched—to ready for the evening.

Or at least she got ready. He glared at the contents of the bag she'd filled with items for him. He pulled out the clothing piece by piece, his annoyance growing and almost snapping at the discovery of not one but two banana thongs.

For those who didn't know the expression, a banana thong was what men, usually with fat bellies, wore to showcase their lack of manhood and balls. The lack of fabric on the bathing suits was appalling, the fact she'd thought he'd wear them even worse.

They hit the garbage can, along with the tight athletic shorts, the mesh crop top, and the T-shirt stating Hot Hunk on Duty.

He did, however, hold on to the few items that weren't completely abhorrent, such as the bright print collared shirts and the khaki shorts. He would have to visit the guest shops at the resort and see what he could do about clothing himself more appropriately.

For now, he kept his current ensemble, the slacks a little more creased than he'd like and his shirt not as fresh as when he'd started the day, but passable enough. He wouldn't be able to continue wearing it on the morrow, though, not with the heat. He'd stick out sorely if he did.

Then again, he already stuck out sorely in this tropical place. People came to these types of places to enjoy themselves. Spend time in the sun. Drink copious amounts of booze. Get laid.

JF hated all those things. Well, except for getting laid. He was a male with needs after all. Needs that shouldn't involve the woman in the room alongside him.

A woman who drove him fucking nuts and they'd not even been together a full day.

Trapped in paradise with a pampered princess.

The horror of it. Why couldn't Gaston have sent someone else and left JF at home?

Most people would have killed for his spot. JF knew that, even understood he was being an idiot for his determination to hate everything happening thus far. But he couldn't help himself. He felt so fucking out of place.

This resort was a place of sunshine and a lack of inhibition. A place people could let their guard down and have fun with no thought of consequences or tomorrow.

However, JF couldn't relax. Relaxing might let the beast within escape. A beast that didn't have very many morals. He might do things, bad things, which would cause trouble.

Only recently he'd seen what happened when those of his kind chose to let hunger and wanton desire overcome good sense. Some of the other soldiers Gaston created had turned on him. Turned on the rules that governed their existence and killed. Killed humans and shifters for food.

Unacceptable for so many reasons.

A whampyr who bucked the rules was a danger to himself and others. Without rules, they hunted without compunction or thought. And when that happened, they died, because Gaston the whampyr savior and creator, couldn't allow his minions to get out of control.

Even without the threat of his maker, JF wouldn't allow himself to falter. He, not the darkness inside, ruled this body.

This mission would test his limits. Test his ability to

look temptation in the eye—instead of below the neck at the exposed valley between her pale breasts—ignore the sweet scent of a woman—honeyed with a hint of vanilla that made his mouth water and his teeth ache—and comport himself as a brother should, protective and glaring, instead of hungry and itching to drag a certain redhead close and see if she'd fit nicely against him.

I already know she's a perfect fit. And I'll bet she tastes divine. Surely one lick wouldn't hurt?

Madness.

"Are you ready, Stoney?" No surprise, she entered his room without knocking.

What would she have done if she caught me doing something dirty? Hopefully joined in.

"Stoney?" he queried.

"Well, I can't exactly keep calling you sweetcheeks. Or did you want to give folks a *G.O.T.* impression of our relationship?" When he blinked at the odd reference, she smiled wide. "Do you not watch *Game of Thrones*?"

"I prefer reading to television."

"Then you should read the first book by George R.R. Martin. All kinds of cool stuff happening in his world and twisted mind. Maybe it will give you ideas. In the meantime, since I don't plan to be Cersei to your Jamie, you need a more appropriate nickname that won't make people think we're doing the wild thing."

"How about just calling me by name? I have one, you know."

"Yes, I know. Jean Francois. Which is much too long. Surely you have something shorter to use. When a woman climaxes and screams, it shouldn't be more than a small mouthful, two syllables at most."

She said the most outrageous things. Two could play that game. "And here I thought women preferred a big mouthful." Her mouth rounded, and he made sure she noticed him staring at her lips when he said, "Open wider."

"You are a very surprising man, sweetcheeks."

"Call me Jean."

"That was my grandmother's name."

Compared to an old woman? His brow furrowed. "Gaston uses JF." Most of his companions referred to him by his initials.

"I am not part of your boys' fraternity. Completely unacceptable. I guess if I must choose something then Francois will do. Although, that is quite French."

"Probably because I am French Canadian."

"Canadian?" Her pitch rose with a hint of incredulity. "I would have never guessed. Canadians are usually such nice people."

"I am nice." He bared his teeth. "I haven't killed anything yet."

She laughed. "The night is young. There's still hope."

With the tinkling bell of her laughter trailing, she exited their room, and he could only follow, lured by the mesmerizing sway of her hips in the much-too-short dress. Could it even be classed as a dress? It barely covered the curve of her buttocks. It clung to every nuance of her shape, enhancing the flare of her hips, the indentation of her waist. As to the front, the plunging vee neckline drew the eye.

It would be so easy to push aside that fabric and nuzzle the skin of her breast.

No nuzzling.

Biting? his inner beast suggested.

Definitely no biting.

Or licking.

Or fondling.

Spoilsport. He couldn't have said which of his inner voices said it.

Dusk had fallen, and yet the resort remained lit, the torches lining the path flickering inside their glass domes, the bulbs within mimicking flames.

He noted other guests, walking in twos or more, most hand in hand, all heading to where the distant thump of a hard bass filled the air.

The pavilion they entered was huge, the massive terrace boasting numerous tables, some large enough to accommodate parties of up to ten people, while smaller two-and four-seat options lined the outer edges.

A massive buffet station held a steady stream of people balancing plates and flatware as they partook of the food and then found a place to enjoy it.

"Be a dear, brother, and fetch us some food while I locate us a spot."

Again with the orders, yet before he could tell her to fetch her own damned vittles, she'd disappeared, her figure sliding gracefully between people, leaving him alone.

Since standing there like a stony rock in the midst of it all would seem suspicious, he headed for the buffet table but only filled up one plate. What he wanted to eat wasn't available on a table or in a warming tray.

With his great height, he could see over most heads and spotted the fiery red crown of his charge. Stacey had, of course, chosen a table in the middle of the action, one packed with people and no room to spare.

He dropped the plate of food with a heavy thump in front of her.

"Thank you."

"You're welcome." Spoken through gritted teeth.

"Everyone, this is Francois, my dear brother."

"Would your brother like to join us?" asked a young fellow—*sniff*—tiger by the smell. The fellow stood and began to move his chair over to make room.

"Don't bother," he muttered. "I'm going to hit the bar." He could handle a few drinks without ill effect. Alcohol didn't affect him much, but unlike regular food, he enjoyed the hot burn of it as it went down his throat.

Leaning against the far edge of the bar, his angle of sight including a direct one to his fake sister, JF looked around and noted all the details he could.

The terrace made of some kind of white stone had several tiers to it. The topmost one, where they were, held the tables and food, plus the first bar. The second tier had comfortable seating, the kind with cushions and small tables to put a drink, circling around a large pool that had a few people swimming in it.

A third tier was narrower in size and then spilled onto the beach. Despite the food on the top level, people milled around everywhere, and of that crowd, a disturbing number were shifters.

Animals masquerading as people.

The predator in him bristled. JF didn't usually mind being amidst shifters. Hell, the club he worked at hired a good number of them and catered to them too. However, when at the club, he was on his turf. With his staff.

Here, he was just another guest. A man outnumbered by pets. But the best part was they had no idea what walked among them.

Shifters couldn't smell his kind. To them, he was a blank olfactory spot. It meant he actually had to resort to wearing scent when out in public lest they wonder too long about it.

Cradling a glass of whiskey—as if he'd debase himself to drink something frou-frou in a bright color—he amused himself by wandering around and identifying the different breeds. There were many.

The most raucous table held all wolves. A rowdy bunch who, if not cut off, would probably start howling and singing.

There were, of course, a large number of lions present. No surprise there considering who owned the resort.

A few tigers, even a pair of foxes who kept to themselves, appeared sprinkled through the mix. And then there were the humans. Lots and lots of humans, many of them staff, but more than a few guests also lacked a shifter scent. It surprised him. He'd expected a resort run by lions to cater only to their type.

Then again, the pride didn't become filthy rich by only serving lions. They knew how to turn a profit.

Still, though, he wondered how often they had to clean up a mess when a drunken shifter accidentally let his beast slip. Did the resort have a special crew for getting rid of pesky human witnesses?

Gaston had a protocol in place for such situations. JF would be more than happy to give the resort a hand if they needed one. Getting rid of bodies was something he specialized in—after he'd taken a bite.

Although it had been a while since he'd had to do anything like that. Once they moved to America, Gaston became very strict about who and what they could eat. In today's modern age, with smartphones taping everyone everywhere, the boss feared the whampyrs getting caught.

Probably a valid concern but it didn't console much when a hollow belly grumbled with hunger. And he'd not eaten before he'd left.

I'll have to go hunting later on. See what he could find in the jungle.

He tossed back the amber liquid in his glass, hearing the silvery bells of Stacey's laughter as she enjoyed herself. He wondered if her gaiety was an act for whoever might be watching, or was this the true Stacey? A party-girl princess. A woman with no inhibitions and morals.

Not that he cared. She wasn't his type, and he wasn't looking to start anything with anyone.

Despite the mild evening, and the half-decent alcohol, JF couldn't stand being surrounded by so much noise and revelry. Not when his hunger made his belly tight.

I need to eat. The guests were off-limits. He'd have to find his blood elsewhere.

As soon as he stepped onto the beach, his shoes sank in the sand. Not exactly the proper footwear for a stroll. It didn't go unnoticed.

"You know, most people usually take their shoes off first before going for a walk." The voice came from behind him. A familiar one. He turned to see Jan, looking fetching in her sarong-style dress, her hair loose and flowing over her shoulders, held back on one side with a flower.

Fetching, and yet she didn't rouse the erotic hunger that Stacey did.

"I don't do barefoot." He'd grown up in a place where winter reigned six months of the year.

"You should try it," Jan teased.

The tone and smile made him frown. Only a completely oblivious idiot would miss the flirting. If only he wasn't immune to it.

Perhaps he should give Jan a chance. After all, she did work here and might provide a clue. Plus, he was hungry. Unlike some of his kind, he knew how to take only a fortifying sip.

"Let me help you." She knelt in front of him, a blonde halo that wouldn't take much to be at the right height to satisfy at least one of his urges.

Jan untied his shoes and slipped them from his feet, tugging his socks after them. Only when she'd gotten him barefooted did she peer up at him. "Isn't that better?"

Truthfully? "The sand's warmer than expected."

"It's been sitting in the sun all day." For some reason, Jan remained on her haunches in front of him, her face almost at the right height. Her eyes bright with interest.

It would be so easy to—

"Brother, there you are." Stacey's voice hit him a moment before her scent did.

A crease of annoyance marred Jan's brow.

"Done partying already?" he asked, tossing the query over his shoulder.

"I'm tired. All that traveling." Stacey covered an exaggerated yawn with her hand. "Walk me back to our room." She didn't ask but commanded.

"I don't think your brother is ready to retire yet. I can have someone take you in a cart," Jan offered.

"No thanks. I only trust Francois to keep my virtue safe. He's so big and strong." Stacey said with a syrupy falseness that even Jan would never believe. "Shall we, brother dear?" Before he could answer, she'd linked her arm in his and tugged him away from Jan.

After a few yards, far enough for them to be out of hearing, especially amidst the sound of the rolling waves, he hissed, "What was that about? I was planning to pump Jan for info."

"I know what kind of pumping she had in mind, and the only oral it involved would have included slurping."

"So what? It's none of your business."

"I don't trust that girl."

At least her instincts were good because neither did he. "Who said anything about trust? She might know things, things I could have found out if not interrupted."

"Or would you have gotten in over your head?"

"I'm not a complete idiot."

"Are you sure? Because experience has shown when men think with their little head instead of the big one, stupid things happen."

"First off, it's not little, and second, I am a grown man, which means if I want to fuck someone, I will, and I don't need your permission." Yet why did talking about fucking a woman other than Stacey make him feel dirty? As if he'd done something wrong.

For some reason, his reply caused her nails to dig into

his arm. "We are here on a mission. Not to hook up with the staff."

"Don't tell me you're jealous?" Surely not, and yet how else to explain her odd reaction to Jan's flirting?

"Jealous? Ha," she scoffed. "You wish. I was just trying to save you from doing something you'd probably regret. A thank you would suffice."

"I always know what I'm doing, so I never regret anything." Except getting involved with the wrong woman a long time ago. A woman who literally tried to rip out his heart. But at least he got a second chance.

"We all have regrets, sweetcheeks. Things we wished we'd done. Things we'd have done differently."

"Dwelling on the past serves no purpose." Ironic, considering his past was why he chose to not get involved anymore.

"I can't say as I disagree about living for today." She danced ahead of him, a redheaded sprite with a bright smile, shoes held in one hand, much like he held his. Him, barefoot in the sand on a beach with a woman. The only things missing were a bottle of wine and a blanket. Because fucking in the sand wasn't good for anyone's delicate parts.

"Given your motto is live for the day, I am surprised you left the party early." He'd wondered if she'd hook up with someone.

I would have killed him.

For what reason?

Did he really need one?

"I stayed long enough to be seen. If our guy was there, he would have noticed me."

"And seen you walking off with me."

"Fear not, I mentioned loudly to everyone in the vicinity that I needed to rescue my brother from a skank looking to get her claws into you."

"You do realize those kinds of remarks will probably make their way back to Jan."

"I should hope so. Maybe she'll get the message and steer clear of you."

"Or else what?"

Vivid green eyes met his. "I refuse to answer on the grounds you might later testify against me."

"You can't kill one of the staff."

"Who said anything about killing? I'm partial to maiming myself. It leaves a lasting impression."

He sighed. "I really hope you're joking." Even as a part of him, the darker part, reveled in her unabashed violent side. A lady with a vicious core. An enticing prize.

"I guess you'll soon find out."

"Does this mean I should gag her when she comes over later for a thorough fuck?" He couldn't have said why he taunted her. What purpose did it serve?

She planted her hands on her hips, and her eyes took on a dangerous expression, and he felt a jolt of desire so strong he almost tackled her to the ground to have his way.

"Don't toy with me, sweetcheeks."

"Or what?" And then, because he could be a dick, he said, "What's that scurrying on the beach behind you?"

"Where? What?" she squeaked, whirling her head. Except the plan backfired as she screamed, "I think it's another spider. They're out to get me!" Stacey flung herself into his arms, staggering him with the unexpectedness of it. Her limbs wrapped around him, ankles locked behind his back, arms looped around his chest.

"There's no spider," he admitted as his free hand cupped her ass and he continued to walk.

"Are you saying that because it's true or because you want to dump me on the ground and force me to face my fear?"

Given they'd reached a dark part of the resort, where the trees loomed close on either side of the path, he did something uncharacteristic. He lied for personal pleasure. "Better hold on tight. I see a few webs along here."

The cheap thrill as she tightened around him anaconda-style was well worth the discomfort of knowing he wasn't immune to her charms.

"So you never asked me why I wanted to go to bed early."

"Because you're tired."

"Of course not, silly. I needed an excuse to get out of there because Melly texted me. She's got some info for us, which means tonight we do some homework. Tomorrow we start working in earnest. Or at least I do. You can keep scowling at everyone and maintaining your cover of over-protective older brother."

"Or I could just head into the jungle where that missing woman was last seen and track down the culprit."

"What makes you think you could find something when no one else could?"

"Because I am just that good."

"I'll be the judge of that." Spoken with a wink.

He adjusted his grip on her, digging his fingers into her ass cheeks, the fleshy part of it, given her dress rode up. "You won't have the energy to judge, let alone think, after." Where she was concerned, the bold remarks just slipped from his lips, and each time, something ignited in the air between them. Something hot. Rife with expectation.

She laughed. "You are something else, Francois." The way she said his name, caressed it with her lips and tongue, made him feels things in a place he'd thought long dead.

Damned whiskey must have given him indigestion because surely he wasn't falling for this pampered princess. She was completely and utterly inappropriate for him.

A wild child to his staidness.

A lioness that wasn't suitable for a whampyr.

A woman that called to his inner beast, and his simmering lust.

A temptation he had to resist.

CHAPTER NINE

WHY IS he so determined to resist me?

She could see he made an effort and yet, at the same time, couldn't completely hide his desire for her. As he'd carried her along—with effortless strength—she'd felt the erection he couldn't hide, pressing against her core. Seen the spark of something in his eyes. Yet, he didn't once try to kiss her or toss her to the ground and have his wild wicked way with her.

Once they reached the better lit part of the path, he finally set her down, and her ass missed the firm grip of his hands. Even more astonishing, he let her walk away. Not a single slap to her behind or whistle at her sassy strut.

How disappointing.

The man was such an enigma. Self-assured. Sparse with his humor and lacking in common sense and taste. Really, he should thank Stacey for saving him from the claws of that simpering Jan. The resort employee obviously saw him as a ticket off this island to better places. Gold digger.

Stacey disliked her with a passion usually reserved only for knock-off brands. Was it any wonder, when she'd seen Jan with Francois, she'd almost pounced her and torn her face off? She'd definitely uttered a very unlady-like growl that caused a few party-goers on the terrace to eye her askance.

Good thing Stacey had a reason to drag him away before he and Jan could drift off into the night doing things that made Stacey's claws pop out without even thinking of it.

Why do I care? No mistaking it bothered her, which could mean only one thing.

I'm jealous. What a novel concept and for a man she didn't even like.

Like his fine body.

Okay, her inner feline had a point. The man was built like a brick house. Having sex with him would be like riding a mountain, all hard ridges and firm thrusting—

Bad kitty. Her mind just couldn't stop veering into naughty places. Perhaps she should get this insane lust for him out of her system. Seduce him, scratch her erotic itch, and then they could both move on.

If I wasn't so preoccupied with Francois and what he was doing, I could cozy up to some male guests and see if they know anything. Or even get close to Maurice. He'd be easy enough to seduce. Francois had a point about pumping the employees for information. Stacey could handle the men, the straight ones at least, while Francois could pretend an interest in the female staff members. Encourage their flirting and...

"Do you hear growling?" he asked from behind her.

"Must be something hunting in the jungle," she snapped, irritated that, once again, he managed to get under her skin.

And this after only one day. She barely knew the man, and yet he irritated her more than that incursion of fleas they'd suffered that year at the lakeside cottage.

Arriving at her room, she slapped her wrist against the door, and it clicked. Pushing it open, she went to enter, only to have Francois butt in ahead of her.

"Manners," she sang. "They're not just for everyone else."

"Stupidity, not just for heroines who shower in haunted houses," he grumbled back.

She blinked as she absorbed the fact that he'd made a joke. Hot damn.

"How is you shoving ahead of me a good thing?" she asked, entering and closing the door.

"I was checking for signs of an intruder."

"I would have smelled one just fine on my own."

"The same way you smell me?"

"I smell you just fine. Although I have to say, Old Spice, aren't you too young for that?"

"It makes me smell human."

"And what do you smell like without it?" Because she'd heard his kind had no scent at all, which to a feline seemed preposterous. Everyone had a scent. A unique one. Surely he did too? Then again, his boss, Gaston, had no scent. But he played with dead things. Probably better no one could smell that.

"Maybe one day I'll let you smell me after a shower."

"Or we could just share a shower. You know, to conserve water."

He didn't reply. Pity. She could have used a sluice off and someone to soap her back.

"The room is clear," he announced. "No signs of tampering."

"I feel so much safer." She held a melodramatic hand to her forehead. "Whatever did I do before you came into my life?"

"I can tell you what I did, not listen to a smartass."

"Thank you."

"For what?"

"Calling me smart. Not everyone recognizes it. They usually just think I'm pretty."

He glowered.

She smiled. "If you'll give me a second to slip into something comfortable, we can read over what Melly sent."

His reply was a grunt, which was why she was perhaps a touch naughtier in her selection of an outfit than she should have been. She emerged from the bathroom wearing simply a short negligee. No panties, no robe, nothing but white silk trimmed in lace.

He still wore his khaki slacks and shirt. And he'd already removed his socks and shoes.

What he couldn't remove was his expression. Had she thought him incapable of anything other than scowls and disapproval?

How wrong. His face remained stony in expression, but his eyes...his eyes smoldered, the depths of them glowing with a red heat.

"Why don't you grab a spot on the couch, sweetcheeks, so we can both read what she sent at the same time."

"I don't mind taking turns."

"Are you afraid of me?" She might have batted her lashes.

A true male could never turn away from a challenge. He sat down hard on the couch, and with a canary-eating grin, she took a spot beside Francois, tucked close against him, her head leaning against part of his shoulder and chest. A rock-hard location, and yet, she found it oddly comfortable.

She held up her phone and then proceeded to enter a series of checks—finger scan, code, another scan, another code.

He sighed. "Is all this subterfuge really that necessary?"

"Melly takes pride security seriously. Let's see what she's got to say."

The first thing to pop up in the report Stacey opened was a brief paragraph. *Found some stuff on the disappearing women. Turns out this has been going on for longer than we expected. At least a few years. The other resorts just haven't advertised it. And it's not just ladies who go missing; sometimes men do too.*

A bisexual predator? Fascinating.

The message went on. *I analyzed the video further. Ran it through some filters and stuff. Couldn't get an identity on the guy, or ascertain if it was a mask or real. But I did spot a few things.*

Being Melly, her message couldn't simply tell Stacey; it showed her.

The video box had a giant triangle that when pressed began to play the clip. The footage was clearer than before, but that wasn't the only modification. When the liotaur entered the clearing, the playback slowed, enlarged, and showed his wrist.

Francois jabbed his finger at the screen. "This is the famous video that sent you here?"

"Yes."

"You do realize it's probably some guy playing a prank."

"Then, if it is, he'll be easy to catch and take care of." She pointed to the liotaur's arm. "He's wearing a wristband."

"Three-quarters of the people on this island are wearing wristbands because they're either a guest or employee. There is no way to tell which resort that band belongs to."

Good point, but she still considered it a clue. The video kept playing, rolling slowly, only enlarging again a moment before the liotaur and his prize exited the screen. The circle around his upper shoulder and a zoom in of the area showed a black smudge.

"He's got a tattoo," she noted aloud.

"Again, describing a fair amount of people."

"Do you have tattoos?" She had to wonder, given he kept himself covered neck to toe. Even his sleeves were long. He'd opted to remain in his clothes rather than those she'd bought for him. Shame. She'd picked up some sweet swimsuits for him.

"Any marks I have on my body are my business, not yours."

"So you do in other words?" She bounced up on her knees. "Show me."

"No."

"Why not?"

"Because I am not a sideshow freak for you to stare at."

"You're going to have to strip eventually."

"If I do, it will be in my room with the door locked."

"Is that a challenge, sweetcheeks?"

"Can we get back to the rest of the report?"

"Chicken," she muttered under her breath. She settled back against him and frowned at the next bit of text. She read it aloud. "There is a very old legend the islanders pass down verbally from generation to generation. It speaks of the lion-headed people who live in the mountain."

"Shifters?" he queried. "It could be the island had some but they died out."

"But they called them lion-headed. Shifters can't do partial shifts."

He disagreed. "Not entirely true. While rare, some shifters can do a partial transformation, keeping their human shape but the rest of their body becoming animal like."

"It is super rare. I mean the most I can do without going all furry is my claws. To do only a head, a complete lion head and nothing else..." Her turn to play devil's advocate. "The more likely scenario is a tribe who hunted lions and used their trophies as headdresses."

"Wearing the head of their kill as a hat?"

"More like a mask, and there is precedent. The ancient Egyptians were big on using animal heads to make themselves seem like gods. But back to Melly's report. Apparently, in the olden days, these lion dudes were considered to be gods and, as such, were given tributes in the form of fresh catches from the sea, fruits and vegetables, and, once a year, the offering of a virgin." She peered up at Francois. "Do you think someone is reenacting the old stories?"

"More like someone is using the old superstitions to get his rocks off. It's a hoax. Some guy obviously thought it would be funny to recreate these supposed ancient gods and is using it to get laid."

"Except people aren't offering the women. He's stealing them."

"Is he really stealing them? The woman in that video isn't really fighting."

"She looks scared."

"Scared and excited. As if she expected something to happen. The fear was probably from being told to run through the woods while something chased her. And when he did, the fear got swallowed by her anticipation."

"You really think this is a hoax? Then why hasn't Shania contacted anyone?"

"It's been how many days since she went missing? Three, four?"

"Three as of tonight."

"It's not too farfetched to imagine she might still be involved in an orgy of the senses."

"A three day orgy?" She pursed her lips. "Who the hell is that good in bed?"

"I once managed three."

The reply startled her to the point she practically fell over trying to crane to see his face.

No smile. No hint of mirth that he teased. Just more of that simmering fire.

"Let's say," she said, trying to not focus on how much stamina a man had to have to manage to keep a woman satisfied for three days straight in bed, "that you're right. That she did go willingly. Where did they go? He's wearing a resort bracelet, and so is she. If they stayed in this resort, someone would have seen her or at least recorded her presence. According to Melly, the bracelets help track the location of guests as they use them on the property. But we haven't had any pings. So if he stashed her somewhere on this property, then he must have removed her bracelet and somehow managed to keep her presence secret while managing to smuggle her in food. Or he was a guest somewhere else and he took her off property to another resort?"

"Or they shacked up at a place in town. Or he stowed her aboard a yacht. Maybe they're even out in the wild camping. At this point all we have are suppositions without any facts."

"Well, at least I'm brainstorming instead of shooting negative nellies at everything I say."

"It's called being the voice of reason."

"I'm a lioness; we're not always reasonable."

"I know. It's why you make awful pets."

She gaped at him. "Did you seriously just relate my kind to that of domestic feline chattel?"

"You're a cat. Cats have owners. It's not that hard to figure out."

One moment she sat next to him, and the next, she straddled him. "Take that back. I am more than just a pussy."

"You're an irrational female who throws herself into things to sate a curiosity that doesn't make room for careful thought or consideration."

"I do believe in your roundabout way that you just called me reckless."

"I did."

She smiled. "Thank you. And because I can't be held accountable for my risky actions..." She pressed her mouth to his. Sealed his lips in a kiss and she was pleased to feel him suck in a breath.

Her breath.

He also didn't shove her away.

Or protest.

So she kept kissing him. Slanting her mouth over his, tasting the firm line of his mouth, the cold and somehow mysterious texture of him that tasted of whiskey and nothing else.

How odd.

Determined to find his true taste, she parted his lips with her tongue, thrusting it into his mouth, sliding it along his. More whiskey, and a hint of something both cold and hot, but still no true flavor.

His hands gripped her ass cheeks, the fingers digging in, and he moved her, rubbed her against him, the turgid proof of his arousal pressing against her, even with his slacks in the way.

No hiding his lust anymore. He wanted her. She wanted him, which meant no way was she stopping.

Her hands gripped the wide strength of his shoulders, feeling the firm flesh. Their tongues danced together, sucking and sliding, while he palmed her ass, grinding her against him.

The frenzy in her built at the friction between their bodies. His lips halted their plunder and trailed across her jaw to her neck. He licked and sucked at her flesh, drawing a moan from her. A shudder clenched her sex as her excitement spiraled.

Down went his lips, blazing a path to the plunging neckline of her nightie. A nudge of his mouth moved the fabric over, baring a rosy tip. He sucked it, drawing it into his mouth, teasing the erect bud with his lips and teeth.

"Yes," she hissed. "Suck it."

He did. He sucked hard at her nipple, pulling it into a point before moving his attention to the other breast. He lavished it with attention, licking and sucking at her flesh, while she squirmed in his lap.

The heat in her boiled, molten desire racing through her veins. Awareness enhancing every touch, moan, and caress.

His lips left her breasts to once again capture her mouth, a hot and fiery embrace that saw her digging her fingers into his hair, tugging at it.

She bounced on his lap, excited. Close to the edge. Needing only a slight push to go over. He once again let his mouth wander, across her jawline to the lobe of her ear. He swirled the shell, and she sighed.

"More," she moaned.

His lips traveled down and paused at her racing pulse. He nipped her neck, sharp enough that she let out a sound.

"That's it, bite me. Bite me hard."

Mark me. Take me.

Instead, he dumped her on the couch and fled faster

than she could blink. Fled through the door separating their rooms, shutting it behind him. Odd.

Did he run to fetch a condom?

Click.

Surely that didn't mean anything. Maybe he had to pee and didn't want her walking in.

She waited.

Waited some more.

But he didn't return.

Well damn. She'd never had a guy run out on her before. Now what? Her sex throbbed. All of her ached with unrelieved passion.

Should I go after him?

And beg he do something about the fire he'd ignited in her body?

Me, beg a man? Not likely.

Only one thing to do when a body screamed for relief and she was too proud to let her fingers do the walking.

Clear night. Hot breeze. Lots of nice smells.

She stripped before stepping out onto the balcony.

CHAPTER TEN

THE MOMENT JF stepped into his room, escaping temptation, he locked the door. Then stared at it, knowing that only a flimsy portal stood between him and *her*.

The woman who, only moments ago, had made him forget himself.

Even now, he could still remember the feel of her in his arms, the taste of her in his mouth. The way she melted at his caresses and demanded more.

Why aren't I giving her what she wants?

Because he'd almost lost control.

He raked fingers through his hair and whirled from the door. He paced the room, every inch of him pulsing, the blood thundering through his veins, molten hot, heating his usually cool skin.

His teeth had pushed from his gums, long and sharp, so sharp he'd nicked her skin. Just a tiny little cut, enough for him to taste a drop.

One. Tiny. Drop.

Just a hint. He'd almost lost his mind.

Almost sank his teeth into her, ready to suck and gulp and drink of her until this ravenous hunger subsided. If she hadn't made a sound, he might have, might have lost control, and then what would have happened?

Pure fucking bliss.

Thankfully, he'd snapped out of it before he did something regrettable and fled.

Fled like a yellow-bellied coward, his insidious mind claimed.

No, like a man who wanted to live another day. If JF lost control and tore out her throat, he might as well slit his own. Between Gaston, his master, and Arik, the lion king, his life wouldn't be worth shit.

Who says you would have killed her? Drinking could be done without damage. A pair of pinprick holes that acted as a straw in a body. But the rules were clear. No eating from shifters, not without permission.

Then there was his personal rule. Don't get involved with shifters. Ever.

The last time hadn't turned out well for him.

How long will I continue to use that one experience as an excuse?

Yes, Sasha turned out to not be who she said. Or what she said. At the time, a mere human, JF had not understood there were other things, hidden things in the world. He'd fallen for the golden-haired girl. A woman who, much like Stacey, ignited his passion. What he didn't expect was that the bubbly exterior hid a monster. A lioness, but one that enjoyed killing for sport.

A seductress who enticed men, human men, into meeting with her, falling for her, so that when she finally changed into her feline beast and struck, they had no defense.

No protection against slashing claws.

No shield against her teeth.

He should have died that night. Would have if Gaston hadn't found him, led to JF's bleeding body by the ghost of another victim.

How well JF still remembered the feel and taste of the blood bubbling at his lips, the coldness settling into his bones. The lack of feeling anywhere. Surely with his body ripped open, he should feel something?

Gaston's eyes had peered into his, serious and, at the same time, full of compassion. He asked him one question, "Do you want to live, no matter the price, that you might avenge yourself and the others who've suffered the same fate?"

Yes. He never knew if he thought the word or if it bubbled past his lips.

It didn't matter. The next time he awoke, he was something new. Different. Stronger.

Inhuman.

He was whampyr, and he got his revenge.

But revenge had never cured his dislike of shifters. Never helped him get over the betrayal of someone he'd thought cared for him.

With years of retrospect under his belt, JF now understood Sasha had played him the entire time, but that was little consolation and didn't help his trust issues with the opposite sex.

They couldn't be trusted.

Ever.

Even if they tasted good. Especially if they tasted

good. Would he remember that it was Stacey in the throes of passion, or would he fall back into that darker nightmare, the one where he woke with blood on his lips and the body of the one who'd betrayed him dead in his arms?

He feared finding out. That, more than his trust issues, was why he'd fled Stacey. Why he locked the door. Why he ignored the throbbing need in his body.

Stripping without care for buttons or folding, or even wrinkles, he dropped his clothes to the floor and fled to the washroom. He thrust his feverish body into the shower and turned on the water. Cold only, yet the tepid spray that emerged did nothing to cool his skin. Nothing to tame his simmering ardor.

She tasted so perfect. Felt so right.

The primal part of him wondered why he didn't go back and claim her. Sex was sex. She offered it. He wanted it. Where was the harm? Even if he couldn't drink her as he wanted to, he could still sink into her velvety depths. Plunge his cock so deep he'd imprint her from the inside.

Fucking madness.

One did not fuck those they'd been sent to guard.

One should never forget she was a shifter. He'd long been taught since his rebirth that they were beneath his kind.

So why can't she be beneath me in bed?

Because.

Just fucking because.

If he had a need, then his hand could take care of it. With that thought in mind, he closed his eyes against the spray and fisted his throbbing cock. Wrapped his fingers tight around it and began to stroke himself. He knew his body, knew how much pressure to apply to the velvet-covered steel length of his shaft. Knew how fast to pump it back and forth.

What he didn't know was why he pictured her, the fiery-haired vixen, her eyes at half-mast, her lips parted. How beautiful she'd look on her knees, lips wrapped around his cock, sucking him. Taking him into her mouth and pleasuring him.

Would he let himself come on her lips, or would he then turn her around and have her present that delectable ass? An ass meant for grabbing as a man fucked her from behind, plunging deep into her velvety folds, thrusting and pumping and...

With a grunt, his cum shot from his cock, and he opened his eyes to see the cold sterile tile of the shower and not her soft expression.

Even worse, he might have shot his load, but his cock remained partially erect. He still wanted her.

Fuck.

He stepped out of the large tiled stall and remained nude, the moisture on his skin pearling, the marks on his body barely visible, silver lines etched into every part of his skin, from his neck down to the soles of his feet. Even his scalp had them. Only his face remained untouched—all the better to walk among the humans unnoticed.

The air conditioning unit chugged along, pushing cold air into the room, enough that, when he stood in front of it, he could feel some of his temperature dropping.

Deep breaths. Eyes shut. Mind blanked. Calmness settled over him.

Until he heard a lion roar, loud and angry.

Then a yowling yelp.

Surely it's not her.

His gaze flicked to the wall separating their rooms.

Don't tell me she's that stupid.

Yeah, she was.

He didn't even take time to throw on clothes, just some boxers, before he shoved open the door between their rooms, and it took only one quick glance to know she'd gone out. The dress on the floor and the open sliding glass doors made that clear. He raced to the door and stepped onto her balcony. The empty balcony that smelled of fresh cat.

I'm going to skin her and make her into furry mittens. Once he found her.

This side of the building had more privacy than some of the others on the resort given it sat on the edge of the jungle. The same jungle that belonged to the conservation land surrounding the volcano. The thick forest boasted tall trees, all of them too far to touch from the balcony, but not far enough for a leap by something agile. Say like a lion.

A part of him was tempted to go back to his room and ignore whatever plight she'd managed to get into. Given her magnetic ability to draw trouble, who knew what she'd run into? Probably another spider. With her princess airs, she might have even simply broken a nail.

Or she'd stumbled into something serious. This wasn't a tamed park of the city. This was a true wilderness with all kinds of peril. Even for a lioness.

Goddamn it. Someone needs to put a leash on that woman.

He launched himself into the air, the change happening quickly, his wings popping free from his back, lightening the bulky part of his body, allowing him to soar high. The change came easily to him now, but it wasn't always like that.

He still remembered the first time he'd transformed, the shock as those monstrous-sized things emerged from his body.

"Where did those come from?" he'd cried at the time.

"They're a part of you now," was the answer. A part of him that hid inside.

As to how he learned to fly? Standing on that rooftop deck, the wind whipping at his new body, the sheer cliff they surveyed dizzying, Gaston had flicked his hands and sent one of his ghostly minions to shove JF over the edge.

When a man was falling, plummeting to a sure death, he learned very quickly to flap the wings at his back.

Even then, he was clumsy and uncoordinated. He almost smashed. Almost, so when he untangled himself from the ground, he ran back up all those stairs to the rooftop, emerging with a scowl and a barked, "What the fuck is wrong with you?

Gaston had beamed, quite proud of himself. "All fledglings need a shove out of the nest," was his apology.

But JF forgave him and then cursed him as he figured out how to draw his new appendages into his back and return to normal. He tried not to think about what his inside must look like with the wings squished in there, the science and magic behind it more than he wanted to know. He did, however, like that, when he needed to, he could fly. A perk to his whampyr state that somewhat made up for the fact that he'd become a monster that needed blood to survive. Drinking blood sure beat dying, though.

Night had fallen, and while the moon sat fat in the sky, a hazy layer of clouds meant it did little to truly illuminate the world below, which suited him just fine. He had no desire for anyone to see or wonder at the dark shape coasting the tropical breezes.

From afar, he might appear as a bat, but up close, his size and very human shape would quickly reveal he was so much more than that.

While he might not enjoy his appearance necessarily —*looking like a fucking gargoyle indeed*—he couldn't deny his increased sensibility to his surroundings. His eyesight, so much sharper. His strength, agility much more concise. As for his hearing, the term "hear a flea fart" came to mind. His ears, pointed and tufted, the shell of them enlarged compared to his human shape, could swivel to a certain extent, listening devices tuned in, looking for a certain sound.

The roar came again, lower in octave this time. Disgruntled and pained.

I'm coming, you dumbass feline.

No wonder Gaston had sent him on this trip. Not even one day here and already she'd managed to get into trouble.

She must have some kind of aura around her that attracts it. How else to explain his own actions?

He banked, a smooth tilt of his wings—that had taken hours of practice to master after his rebirth—and skimmed the tops of the trees, peering through the branches to the ground below. He almost passed her by.

A hint of gold caught his eye, and he pulled up to slow his passage.

For a moment, he hovered overhead, big wings flapping slowly, using the currents to hold him aloft, trying to catch that glimpse of gold again. "Where are you?" he muttered.

"Meowr. Grawr." The feline complaint came from below and to his left.

With her location pinpointed, he lowered himself until his feet gripped a thick bough. Then as he peered through leaves and shadows to truly locate her, he shook his head and said, "You've got to be fucking kidding me." He'd found Stacey, and a good thing too. She'd gotten herself into quite the bind.

Walking along the branch with perfect balance, he hopped from it to one lower then another until he was on a thick bough, wrapped with a rope. From that rope dangled a lioness caught upside down in a snare.

"I've heard of cat caught your tongue, but really, a tree catching a cat?" He crouched down and got to enjoy the way her amber eyes snapped. Despite not being an animal lover, he admired the smooth sleek appearance of her fur. The toned muscles of her limbs.

"Growr," she snarled.

"Don't get pissy with me, princess. I'm not the one who left the safety of our room to roam a strange forest and was reckless enough to get caught by a simple hunter's trap."

"Meowr."

"Yes, it was dumb."

Hiss. Glare.

He finally smiled for the first time this trip, which she

might not realize was a smile, given his hybrid shape tended to sport a heck of a lot more teeth.

"Would you like me to help you?"

She nodded her furry head.

"Say please."

Despite her feline form, she managed a very distinct dirty look.

"I don't know why you didn't just shift shapes. It's only a simple knot."

"Meowrrrr." She yowled and wiggled in the snare. It was then he noticed the glint in it, a glint of silver, not just regular rope.

"Well, I'll be damned again, this is a trap meant for a shifter. You can't change back, can you?"

She shook her head.

Silver on its own wasn't pleasant to shifters, but something in the metal didn't agree with the mechanism for shifting. Add a hint of magic to it, because, yes, magic did exist, and silver could do many things, such as prevent a lioness from becoming a woman.

"Hold on, princess. I'll get you out of there." Crouching down on the branch, he used his claws to pull at the strands, hissing as the silver strands, imbued with something, something Gaston would probably recognize, burned his skin. The fact that it affected him too, a whampyr, not a shifter, wasn't something he wanted to dwell on. He was perfectly happy with his snobby view of the world and its inhabitants.

The rope frayed, and before it could snap, he grabbed a hold of it. With only a little effort, he heaved the rope, ignoring the burning on his palms, until he had Stacey on the branch beside him. The lioness had no problem balancing on the limb, and he quickly pulled the tight noose off her hind leg. A ring of burned fur remained behind. Fur that turned into red and blistered skin on a pale ankle.

"Poop on a stick, that hurt," she protested.

"Then maybe you shouldn't have stepped in it."

"I wasn't expecting any traps. That was unbelievably rude of whoever left that there." Her gaze lasered the offensive rope before she kicked it off the branch.

He didn't watch it go, more fascinated by the naked woman before him. So unbelievably sexy it almost hurt.

"What were you doing out here?"

"Blowing off steam."

"Alone, in the woods, at night, with a known predator kidnapping women? Were you dropped on your head as a child?"

"I always land on my four feet. In my defense, who'd expect a trap in the middle of nowhere? Maurice told me the volcano was a good place to explore."

"Maurice is a puny excuse for a predator who probably couldn't catch a mouse."

"Speaking of mice..." She eyeballed him. "You kind of look like a giant mouse with wings."

"Are you fucking with me?" He straightened and crossed his arms. "I am nothing of the sort."

"Would you prefer I call you a bat?"

"Not particularly. I am whampyr, which is nothing like either of those two animals."

"Have you looked in a mirror? If it looks like a bat, flies like a bat, then it probably is a bat. Just a bigger sized one."

"I should have left you upside down."

"Is that a hint you prefer me from another view?" She popped to her feet and did the unthinkable. Bent over, pushing her ass into the air, and giving him a shadowy peek at what lay between her legs.

Lick it.

No licking.

But she's offering.

Still not licking.

"I can't believe I'm losing sleep for this," he grumbled.

"I can't believe you're not trying to take advantage of me." A reply given as she peeked between her legs.

"Desperation isn't attractive."

"Excuse me!" She unfolded herself and whirled to face him on the branch. "I am not desperate."

"So you say, yet you keep trying to throw yourself at me."

"Why, I never," she huffed.

"And you never will." Best he put a stop to this right now because he could feel his blood boiling again. Being near her, especially with her naked and flushed, did something to his cold control. Something that made his usually sluggish heart beat faster.

Did she know how dangerous her teasing could be? Had no one ever taught her not to tempt monsters bigger than her?

"Never say never, sweetcheeks. Especially to a lioness."

"This isn't a game," he growled. "You have no idea who you're messing with."

"Ooh, look at me shaking in fear at the big bad whampyr."

"You should. I'm capable of things you can't even imagine."

"Like making arrogant statements."

"You're impossible," he snapped.

"But doable." She smiled. "Even your boxers can't hide that." Her gaze dropped, and that was it. He couldn't handle it anymore. Couldn't handle *her*.

She kept teasing and tempting the beast. At one point, he would snap. Before that could happen, he fled.

Climbing branch to branch, nimble and fast, until he emerged from the tree top and could take flight. Throwing himself into the warm currents coming off the ocean, he meant to escape her, only to find himself circling back, high enough overhead that she couldn't easily spot him, but with his keen eyesight, he watched. He watched her as she made her way back through the jungle, once again wearing her fur, her steps ginger, cautiously testing the ground lest another trap find her.

Only once he saw her reach the safety of her room did he spiral away, a primal cry rising from his chest, bursting free.

A cry that was answered by something off in the distance in the jungle.

Time to hunt.

CHAPTER ELEVEN

BRIGHT and early the next day, Stacey had a decision to make. Breakfast in bed, or breakfast in his bed?

Guess which she chose.

Except upon entering his room—the lock he'd engaged no match for a determined lioness—she found his bed empty. It did look slept in, though, which meant he'd returned at one point the previous night, but where oh where could sweetcheeks have gone? Running water gave her a clue.

She threw herself on his bed to wait, and when the bathroom door opened, releasing a billow of steam, she smiled at him.

"Good morning!" Said with all the brightness of the dawning sun.

"Go away." Said with the dark thunder of a cloud set to rain on her day.

He tried to step back in the bathroom, but she sprang from the bed, stalking his steps, giving him no room to escape. As if she'd let him go. He wore only a towel, low hanging on lean hips, his upper body—and what an upper body!—bare and moist from his bathing.

It made her thirsty, and everyone knew how cats liked to drink.

I wonder what he'd do if I gave him a lick. And not just a lick meant to quench her thirst.

"Would you stop staring?" he grumbled.

Not happening. When presented with a splendid specimen of a man, it was her duty as a nubile female to stare.

While she ogled, she asked questions. "What's up with your skin?" She reached out to touch, a jolt of awareness that caused her to suck in a breath. He didn't move, which surprised her. Despite the rigid tension in his frame, he let her fingers trail over him, tracing the whorls and sigils in silver relief all over his body. "Are those scars?"

"No."

"Tattoos?"

"They're not technically manmade, if that's what you're asking."

"You mean this is natural." Startled, she glanced at his face. "These designs are awfully intricate for simple genetics."

"No more complicated than stripes on a zebra or coloration on a peacock."

"Those animals don't turn into something else."

"If you're asking if this is a whampyr trait, then yes. We all have them."

"And they're all over your body?"

"Mostly, except for hands, neck, and head. Some of

my kind have fewer markings than others. It's considered a level of strength the more you're covered."

"The more design the merrier, in other words," she mused aloud. She couldn't help but walk around him, noting the lines looping and swirling across his back, down the line of his spine and disappearing under his towel. "I thought I saw some markings when you were in your whampyr shape last night. But they were harder to see. Not silver like they are now."

"The marks remain no matter our shape. They just get darker when we transform."

"Do they mean anything?" she asked, because, despite his claim they were a natural characteristic, something about them seemed to speak to her. A language in need of deciphering.

"The pattern on our skin is only that, a pattern, nothing more. No whampyr shares the same pattern. Each of us bears a distinct mark. Like a fingerprint to a human."

"Were you born like this?" A lioness could no more contain her curiosity than she could resist the urge to roll in a patch of catnip. And it was a valid question. Despite popular human belief, shifters were not created. They were born. Two parents preferably, but mixed couples had been known to birth too. They also tended to throw some latent shifters into the general population.

"I did not start out my life as a whampyr." Stark. Meant to halt the line of questioning.

But she wasn't done. "So you were made."

"Made. Created. Transformed. The details of it are none of your business."

Did he not yet grasp she was making him her business?

Leaning close to him, her breath brushing his back, she murmured, "Haven't you figured it out yet? Making this hard for me only makes it harder on you, because I always get what I want."

"Not this time, princess."

"Oh yes I will. Consider this fair warning, I am not afraid to torture you."

"You can't hurt me."

"Who said anything about pain?" She pressed her lips against his skin, feeling that amazing jolt of awareness again. It hit her right between the legs, starting a pulse in her sex that had her boldly pressing herself against him.

Leaning into his back, she pressed her cheek against the bare skin there. Her arms wrapped around his front, hands splayed across his taut abdomen.

"What are you doing?"

"What's it feel like I'm doing?" Her hand drifted down, over the ridge of the towel, stroking over his terry-cloth-covered thighs.

"Stop it."

"Tell me what I want to know."

"I won't."

A hand brushed over the bulge between his thighs, the one pushing at his towel. Wanting to say hello. "Tell me how you were made."

Instead, he whirled, grabbing her and forcefully pushing her up against the bathroom wall, his eyes blazing with red fire. His lips twisted in anger. "I said enough. We are not doing this."

"Yes, we are." Confidence was a woman's best friend.

"There are things you don't understand about me."

"Then tell me. Tell me and I'll stop."

"You'll stop because I say so." He tried to sound bossy.

"What's the big deal? Why is how you became a whampyr such a secret? This has to do with Gaston, doesn't it? Oh my God." Her eyes widened. "Are you a zombie? Did he like bring you back to life?"

"How the fuck does your mind work? Do I feel dead?"

"No." Most definitely not, although his temperature didn't run as hot as a shifter. "But Gaston is a necromancer and your master."

He sighed. "I am not dead. Although I came close. Gaston saved me, but in order to do so, he had to transform my human body into something else."

"He did this with magic?" She trailed her fingers over him and felt the trace shiver in his body.

"Magic. Necromancy and ingredients that he won't ever reveal. It is an ancient secret and one he doesn't use lightly. Not everyone survives the spell."

"But you did, because you're strong." So strong and not just in body, but mind. He had an indomitable will that she found extremely appealing. "How did you almost die?"

"You won't like the answer."

Perhaps not, but she had a feeling it would answer a lot about him. "Tell me."

"A woman. A lioness shifter, just like you, eviscerated me."

"What?" The reply shocked her. "Did you do something to piss her off?"

"How nice of you to automatically assume I did something wrong."

"We don't kill wantonly. Not humans at least."

"Sasha did. She left a trail of bodies in the cities she visited. Gaston found me before I completely bled out."

"What happened to the woman?"

A slow, cold smile pulled his lips. "She died."

"You killed her? And no one retaliated?" Shifters didn't condone violence against their own.

"I was even rewarded for it. Apparently, Sasha had been infected with some form of madness. A rabies for shifters."

Rare and incurable. "A kill order was enacted," she said, finishing his story. "Well, I guess that explains a lot about you."

"Do you see why I want nothing to do with you or your kind?"

She blew a raspberry. "Oh please. You're not going to tell me that's your lame excuse. It happened ages ago, and I am obviously not a psychopathic killer."

"The jury's out on that one."

"I have no plans to kill you." Then, because she was a biatch, she added, "Yet."

"I'm no longer a weak human with tender skin. So go ahead and try."

"And get blood all over my frock?" She looked down at herself. "Let me at least take it off first." She grabbed the hem, only to have him slap her hands away.

"Don't you dare get naked."

"Why not?"

"Just don't," he growled.

She didn't need to ask why again. She could see it in the red glint peeking from his eyes.

He wants me, but he doesn't want to want me.

Adorable. "Shut up already and kiss me."

"No."

"I'm afraid I don't recognize that word." Not with him.

She grabbed his face and pulled it close enough to take his mouth. Take it and revel in the feel of it moving against hers. The mintiness of his toothpaste masked his true flavor, but she didn't care because she kissed him. And despite his words, his anger at her kind, he embraced her back.

A low groan escaped him as he gave in to the passion that erupted between them, his mouth hungrily devouring hers, and when his sharp teeth nicked her lower lip, releasing the coppery tang of blood, she moaned.

"Yes. More."

This time, he didn't stop. He suckled at her lower lip, drawing more of that blood, setting every nerve inside her on fire.

His hands stroked down the fine linen of her dress, cupping her ass through the fabric, squeezing those cheeks.

His big body pressed in against her, the hardness of his erection barred entry by the towel and clothing they both wore. But she felt it. Felt it pulsing and pushing, his desire for her evident.

That same intense arousal coursed through her, demanding satisfaction.

She reached between them, tugging at his towel, loosening it enough that she could grasp the root of his erection. His thick erection.

Goodness. The size of it would stretch her. Pummel her soft flesh. Her channel squeezed in excitement, and her fresh panties grew damp. All of her throbbed with desire. Need.

"Take me," she whispered. "I need—"

Knock. Knock. Knock.

"Ignore it," she murmured, feeling him freeze.

"Someone is here."

"Probably room service."

"Which means if we don't answer, they will come in." He pushed away from her, catching his towel before it could completely hit the floor. He rewrapped it around his hips as he left the bathroom.

Left her aching and frustrated.

"Who is it?" she heard him bark as she smoothed her hair and took a few breaths to calm her racing pulse.

A muffled reply. "It's me, Jan."

The little whore was back to make another attempt. Like hell.

He's mine.

Before Stacey could roll her eyes at the brazen hussy starting so early, he'd opened the door.

In his towel.

The man had no common sense whatsoever.

Stacey's gaze narrowed on the woman in the doorframe, who dared to look fresh and inviting in her form-fitting khaki shorts, blouse tied off at midriff, and was that a belly button piercing glinting? Francois shifted, blocking Stacey from Jan's sight.

Smart man. He knew better than to agitate Stacey's lioness. He probably wanted to get rid of Jan quickly so he could return to their interrupted passion.

Any second now, Francois would slam the door.

Any second...

Still waiting.

"Morning," gruffly said by Francois to Jan, and yet it was more than he'd offered Stacey.

The jerk. Trying to make me jealous.

Totally working.

"Sorry for the early visit," said syrupy Jan. "But I wanted to tell you we had a cancellation for our volcano tour that leaves shortly, and I wondered if you'd be interested."

Interested? I know what you're interested in. A piece of Francois.

Time to put a stop to it right now. Stacey sidled up behind Francois, who did a good job of blocking the doorway, and peeked around his bare arm. "How nice of you to offer. A jungle trek sounds like just the thing to get our trip started."

Pale blue eyes met hers, the coldness in them startling and gone as quickly as it came. An apologetic look crossed Jan's face. "I'm sorry. We only have room for one more person. It's a very popular tour and only has limited spots."

Of course the little slut only had room for one. Whatever. Francois would probably turn her down. He was here to protect her—and he had a fire to put out between her legs.

But the jerk surprised her again. "Is this the one the bartender was talking about?"

"Yes. It's quite popular with the more adventurous males at the resort."

"I'm in."

He was what?

"What do you mean you're in? What happened to spending time together?" What happened to him putting his face between her legs and taking care of the honey pooling there for him?

"I am pretty sure you'll manage to keep yourself entertained for a few hours."

"But who will rub the lotion on my skin? I burn easily." Said more petulantly than she liked.

"You can always ask for help from the staff. We're here to please." Spoken by Jan as she stared at Francois.

I know that look. Stacey used that look, the kind that said anything you want, you big hunk of manly love, you can have. Naked.

But Jan was using it on Francois, and he wasn't looking away, and no one was paying attention to Stacey.

Pounce them both. Her inner lioness took issue with the flirting between Francois and Jan.

Jealousy made her claws try to poke. Jealousy combined with frustration made her want to scream.

His attitude, and general actions, pissed her off.

Which, in turn, slapped her awake.

What am I doing? Why do I care? It wasn't even as if she really liked him. Despite what happened in the bathroom, and even the day before, she wasn't interested in Francois. Not one bit. Sure, she wouldn't mind a fun and sweaty romp, but long term? Never.

His hands were much too callused for boyfriend

material. Hard and ridged and they'd probably scrape something fierce across her skin.

Shiver.

Would she ever find out, or would he run his deliciously big hands over Jan's skin?

I'll eviscerate the whore.

Whoa. She shoved her jealousy into a hole and told it to shut up. She wasn't about to become one of those women who couldn't handle a guy choosing someone else. And who said this wasn't part of his plan?

On second thought, this entire flirtation he had going with Jan probably had to do with their mission. *He's acting.* Because, hello, no way he'd prefer that boring blonde to a redhead.

His pretend interest in Jan would work out well, providing a good opportunity for Francois to discover something while getting him out of her way so she could begin doing her own investigating.

"Go with Jan. I'll be fine," she said with a smile much too bright. "You'll have tons of fun."

"I'm not doing this for fun."

"I'm sure it will be awful, and you can scowl the entire time. But be a dear and get some pictures, why don't you?"

"When does it leave?" he asked Jan.

"In thirty minutes from the main clubhouse."

"I'll be there." He slammed the door shut and waited, they both did, as Jan's steps receded. Only then did he whirl on her. "Were you trying to blow our cover?"

"What are you talking about?"

"The way you were cock blocking me there."

"You're not actually thinking of getting with that skank, are you?"

"She's not a skank."

"You're not seeing it because you're thinking with the wrong head."

"Who I fuck with is none of your business."

"It is totally my business." She kept talking and couldn't quite seem to control the possessive words coming out of her mouth.

He noticed. "You sound more like a freaking girl-friend than a sister."

"I am just a concerned observer."

With slow steps, he moved toward her. "What game are you playing, princess?"

"No idea what you're talking about. Unless you mean *Clash of Clans*. I have to check on it daily to collect my stuff."

"Don't pretend to be stupid. I'm talking about your attitude with me."

She batted her lashes. "Whatever are you talking about?"

He stopped in front of her, a big, menacing presence, still half naked. So tempting.

She placed her hand on his chest. Felt the oddly slow beat of his heart. A beat that split into two and the flesh under her fingertips warmed. "In spite of what just happened, princess, we are not a thing. I have no interest in you."

"Would you like me to prove that statement wrong?" Said tersely. She didn't like the fact that he denied what happened.

"I am not some toy you can play with. I don't belong to you."

"I should hope not. No one should ever belong to another person." But borrowing on the other hand... *He can borrow my body any time he likes.* Her fingers trailed up his chest, tracing along his jaw, rubbing over his lips, the tips of them pressing against his incisors. His eyes glinted with red.

"Stop that."

"Make me."

"You're playing with fire, princess."

"Ever think that maybe I want to burn?"

He pulled her hand from him. "Try to stay focused."

"I'd probably focus more if we had sex."

"I'm sure the resort could arrange something if you're that hard up. Although I imagine you could crook your finger by the pool and summon the stud of your liking."

"Are you really telling me to go screw another man? Is that what you want?" She couldn't help an incredulous tone.

"I don't care what you do."

Said with a straight face, and yet her inner lioness immediately growled, *lie.* "You really don't care?"

"No."

"So the thought of my hands running over another man's body doesn't bother you. You'd be okay with some other dick slipping into the heat you started." She cupped her mound through her dress and noticed him staring.

"Stop it," he growled.

"Stop what? You're not supposed to be bothered by the idea of another man licking my skin. Or my mouth—"

"Enough!" he roared. "I don't want you fucking anyone else. Is that what you want to hear?"

"Yes."

He slashed a hand through the air. "It means nothing. We are here on a job, so how about you focus on why we're here and keep your libido and hands to yourself?"

"That's no fun."

"Exactly. We're not here for fun."

She sighed. "Anyone ever tell you that you're a spoil-sport?" And a pussy tease.

"All the time."

"Are you really going to leave me alone for the day? You do realize that you were sent to keep me out of mischief."

"Are you threatening to misbehave if I go?"

"Threaten? Me? I'll be acting like myself. Not my fault if some people are offended by it."

"Can you manage to not land in jail for one day? I'd rather not use up my cash to bail you out."

"Does this look like the face and body of a woman who spends time in jail?" She gestured to her elegantly attired frame.

"I hear the pride has great lawyers."

She laughed. They did, which was why the biatches got out of more fiascos than most.

"I'm not going to change your mind, am I?" Stacey said.

"Nope."

"Fine. Go on the little road trip with Jan. See how much the little slut tells you."

"And what will you do?"

"I shall plan a wedding and, at the same time, question people," while attempting to not turn into a lobster. Good thing she'd brought that box with her military-grade sunscreen. Bought from a scientist selling secrets from NASA, it was strong enough to protect her even from UV rays beamed at her from an alien planet.

"Stay out of trouble." He wagged a finger.

She almost bit it.

"I will promise to be good for a kiss." Bargaining for sexual favors. A new thing for her.

But it worked.

He drew her close, of his own volition this time. He pulled her up on tiptoe, his lips a hairsbreadth from hers. So close she could feel his breath.

He murmured, "You want a kiss, then be good until I get back."

A whole day without getting into mischief?

That would be a challenge.

Before she could ask for a preliminary taste, he whirled from her and began to dress.

In short order, Francois was gone, and Stacey was left to her own devices. She opened the package with her special sunscreen, a giant keg of it. With Francois gone, there was no one to tote it around for her, so she tucked it under one arm but didn't have to go far before a male offered to carry it for her. The little foxy French dude from overseas grabbed it, grunted at its weight, and dropped it. On his toe. His screams brought other guests.

The next two fellows struggled with the keg too.

Weaklings. She missed Francois and his strong arms already.

Those arms better not hug anyone else. Or she'd rip them off and beat him with them.

CHAPTER TWELVE

IN TRUTH, JF didn't want to go on a stupid fucking tour. If he wanted to explore the volcano, he'd do it himself by air where he'd cover more ground. Problem was he wouldn't see much at night, and before he began flying over it during the day, he wanted a better idea of what to expect.

Logic, however, didn't make him any happier, not given he was jounced about in a fucking truck, which could have brought along Stacey if Jan wasn't determined to glue herself to his side.

The annoying female wasn't necessary to the tour, something he realized not long after their departure. Jan commandeered the seat beside him in the all-terrain vehicle, a modified pickup truck. In the bed of it, two rows of benches with roll bars overhead. Each bench sat four people, all men. All shifters. The benches could have squeezed one or two more.

But then again, probably best they didn't. As it was, JF was getting too close to Stacey.

Too hungry for her.

If Jan hadn't interrupted this morning, how far would things have gone?

All the way, the beast replied with a dark laugh.

JF had mistakenly—no, he'd purposely nicked her lip for a taste. It only made things worse. Now he truly knew how sweet she tasted. He wanted more.

Drink up, buttercup. His inner monster didn't have any qualms.

How long could he hold out if she kept insisting?

Not long if she attacked him with kisses again.

I need to stay away. Keep himself out of temptation's reach. Away from those luscious lips.

What of my promise to her? The one he'd made promising her an embrace if she behaved. Probably nothing to worry about. No way would Stacey go an entire day staying out of trouble.

She was trouble with a capital T. The woman needed a keeper. A man to watch over her and punch out those that might take offense at her princess airs.

I should have stuck close to her.

He looked back in the direction of the resort. They hadn't gone too far yet. He could jump out and make it back within an hour.

The mere fact that he calculated it meant he deserved the mental slap.

The strange urge he had to watch over her was why he had to escape. Why he'd chosen to embark on this lame jungle adventure.

Stay away. Far away. Even if bored and tortured by a desperate woman.

Give the expedition a chance. Maybe he'd learn something.

Yeah, like where to hide a body on this island.

Hehehe.

The front cab of the truck held a driver and a partner who read off a script as they drove through a rutted track in the jungle. A history of the island, which he tuned out, much like he tuned out the woman beside him.

Jan babbled, and he grunted and nodded every so often, only partially listening. Not once did the bubbly blonde reveal anything he needed to know. Such a waste of air, so he interrupted her to ask a question.

"I thought the volcano was on protected land." And yet here they were supposedly driving to see it.

"It is. However, you can't really expect people to ignore it's there. The government and enforcement agencies turn a blind eye to small expeditions that go in to take a peek. So long as we don't create any new trails or destroy anything, they don't really care."

"And we're actually going to the volcano?"

"The base of it at any rate. The sides of it are pretty sheer. You'd need to be a spider monkey to climb them."

He tossed out some of the lore he'd learned from Stacey. "I heard there was some kind of cult that used to worship the volcano."

"They weren't a cult." Said with vehemence.

"You've heard about them?"

"More than heard. I studied them when I came to the island. They were the basis of my cultural thesis. They were more than a cult. The Lleyoniias"—spoken with a hint of a drawl—"were here before any of the human islanders. They were an ancient race of gods."

"Gods don't exist."

"Or do they simply choose not to show themselves to you?"

"How can you believe without proof?"

"I've studied the proof. Seen the history and the pictures."

"Pictures?" He snorted. "Men wearing lion heads."

"You're describing one way they've been depicted. Apparently, they were lions. Shapeshifters, but of a more advanced sort than we see today," she added softly, with an eye on the other tourists. Given their scent placed no humans among them, he wasn't sure he understood her caution.

"Maurice says the island population is all human now. Did these god fellows die out?"

"The stories are murky on that point. Some say the islanders refused to give the Lleyoniias a part of their bounty, and when invaders came, the gods left with them on their ships. Other legends state the volcano erupted and wiped them out."

"No matter their fate, their legends live on. What do you think happened? Do you think they all died out, or have they simply been in hiding?"

"I think that it's an interesting story." She smiled. "But I'm much more interested in you. What are you?" A direct question.

"I don't know what you mean."

"You're not a shifter."

"You are correct. I am not."

"But your sister is one. Surely you carry the gene too."

"Alas, it skipped me. I'm just a simple man."

She shook her head. "You're lying. You might not be shifter, but you're also not human. You have marks on your body."

Denying it was pointless. They were hard to hide, but that didn't mean he had to spill what they meant. "What I am is none of your business."

"What if I want to make it my business? As an employee of the resort, I am obligated to find out if you might pose a risk to other guests."

"So long as they leave me alone, they're fine."

"Not good enough," was said with a shake of her head. "You can't expect me to take you at your word. The fact you keep adamantly refusing is rather suspicious."

"Because it's none of your fucking business." It took control to not let the angry beast rise to the surface and give her a hint of what he was.

For a young woman, she proved awfully pushy, but Jan would find that he didn't care what her sex or age was. If she shoved too hard at him, JF would shove back.

The truck jolted to a stop as their guide hopped out of the front and advised them they'd now keep moving on foot.

It was with more wariness than before that JF followed, noting how Jan stayed behind the group. He glanced at her from time to time, wondering at her sudden distance from him, noting how she watched the forest. So when the ambush came, he was ready.

The wild boar came racing out of the jungle, a group of them, their bodies big and bulky, their coarse hair striated for better camouflage. Their eyes focused on the invaders to their territory. They uttered loud snorts and snuffles as they ducked their heads to charge, leading with their sharp and ragged tusks.

"Can we?" asked one of the guests, fingers on the buttons of his shirt.

"Go right ahead. Humans aren't allowed in this sector," answered the guide.

The men of the group scattered, excitement firing their veins. He could hear their shouts as they stripped and ran, the excitement of the chase, which would turn into a hunt, a vivid battle cry that rose all around him. When presented with another predator, one that threatened and promised a good fight, shifters couldn't help themselves, the call to their more primal side too hard to ignore.

So they left, and the jungle filled with the catcalling sounds of feline predators at play.

Only the guides, Jan, and JF remained clothed and by the truck.

"Aren't you going to hunt with them?" the driver asked.

"I think I'd prefer to explore the volcano instead."

"Then you'll want to go that way." The guide pointed but didn't offer to lead him.

Not that JF needed help, but he was surprised Jan didn't comment.

Perhaps she'd finally given up on her obsession with him.

He took off in the direction the guide recommended but veered slightly from the main path once he saw the secondary trail someone had tried to hide, the big fat leaves too carefully positioned to be natural. Pulling them to the side revealed a less used option. The odd thing about the second faint track was the lack of scent.

No odor at all. Almost as if someone had tried to hide it. *Or make it seem as if a whampyr had left it.*

Just because shifters couldn't smell them, though, didn't mean whampyrs lacked a smell. Theirs just resided on a more esoteric level. Another whampyr could *scent* it; it just took a little more effort.

JF let only a part of himself change, a peek of the beast to truly inhale and filter the air around him.

Still nothing—

Wait. A hint of chemical. Something manmade and unnatural. To what purpose? Had someone intentionally neutralized all scent?

Interesting. And why do it other than to hide something?

Secrets. Always with the secrets.

Although he now had one less secret with Stacey. *I can't believe I told her what happened to me.*

Told her and tried to find the anger to hate her. It was because of her kind he'd more or less died.

But it wasn't her.

However, she had some of the same brash nature. The same violent tendencies.

I'm more violent too. He definitely wasn't a man that could be pushed anymore.

Sasha was an anomaly. A sick lioness. Stacey wasn't sick. Hot, sexy, and frustrating, yes, but she was the cure to what ailed him.

But would she also be what brought about his downfall? When he was with her, he lost all control. All common sense fled. What if he didn't hold on tight enough and the beast took over?

Maybe I should buy myself a pink fucking dress and start talking in a high-pitched voice about my fucking feelings. What the hell was wrong with him? Mooning over a goddamned princess.

Fuck her and get over it.

He'd just have to be sure he didn't bite her again. No biting. Just hot and sweaty sex.

Speaking of sweat... The heat of the jungle made his linen shirt stick. He'd opted for a muted print shirt, long-sleeved, plus slacks he'd ordered from a shop in town. Maurice had made the arrangements. As if he'd wear the crap Stacey had packed for him.

Reaching the base of the volcano, he paused and looked up, noting the jagged sides, black and gray chunks with scraggly greenery struggling to push through. Not conducive to climbing. Although an agile person could probably make it to the dark ledge he noticed partway up.

It would be easier to fly.

But he didn't dare right now. Who knew who might be watching? He also wondered if there was any point. The second path he'd followed led to a dead end. Perhaps this place meant nothing.

He certainly couldn't smell anything out of the ordinary. Not a single scent of human or shifter. Just flowers and foliage, along with the older musky scent of wild boar.

With his hands shoved in his pockets, he strode closer to the base of the mountain, eyes scanning a dense curtain of shrubs. Extremely dense, and yet he spotted—

"Oink!" The loud pig sound had him jerking his gaze

to the left in time to see a tusked boar charging from the woods, squealing.

If only he were here alone. It would make a great al fresco lunch, but keeping his secret was more important.

No flashing the monster in public.

Agility, though, wasn't just for his whampyr shape. JF eyed the charging boar, timing his leap. Once he landed behind it, he'd have to move fast. He'd have to wrestle it with his bare hands since he'd not brought a weapon.

Intent on the charging pig, he didn't react when he heard a whir. A moment later, an insect nipped him, a sharp bite to his neck.

Ouch. He didn't dare raise a hand to slap it. Not with the boar only paces away.

Another insect nipped him in the butt. Seriously?

The distraction took his eyes from the boar hurtling at him. He dodged to the side, but his body felt sluggish, slow.

Clumsy.

He stumbled. And fell—

CHAPTER THIRTEEN

WHERE IS JF? The day took forever to pass. Stacey had spent her morning checking out the resort, every nook and cranny, with Maurice at her side explaining the amenities available for a wedding. He'd answered every single question posed without hesitation. Let her peek into every single corner and cupboard she wanted. To find nothing.

After lunch, she took a different tact, embarking on a sailing boat with other guests. Throwing up over the side and going back to shore. Cats and water did not mix.

She spent the rest of that afternoon by the pool, pumping people for information while, at the same time, pumping handful after handful of cream to keep her skin from turning into red-seared steak. Those who slathered her, talked. And talked.

Everything she learned proved boring. So boring, even with all the tropical drinks.

By late afternoon, she was greasy, frustrated, and had nothing to show for her day of investigation.

Okay, not entirely nothing. A few people talked about the missing girl, in terms of either "Oh my God, hope she's okay" to "Wonder who she shacked up with."

No one seemed unduly concerned they themselves could go missing. The resort did its best to act as if everything was okay. This was a place of fun and adventure, not fear.

Bo-o-r-r-r-ing. She wanted to shake things up. Really was tempted to do something, anything, to relieve her irritation.

But then Francois might not kiss me.

Since when did that matter? Since when did she behave for a man?

Since I found one that makes me feel all mushy inside. How long since she'd met a fellow who evinced more than a passing interest from her? JF didn't fawn over her. Didn't say yes to everything she demanded.

The man had a backbone, and it was damned sexy.

Everything about him was so freaking hot. *And I want it all.*

Want him.

Was she falling for the guy? She barely knew him. Yet, the more she discovered, the more he intrigued.

At least now she understood why he acted so disparaging to her and the other lions. He'd been hurt. Hurt badly. She could see how he'd have trust issues. See it, but not understand it because she'd never truly suffered like Francois had. Raised as a pampered princess, the youngest of the brood, Stacey enjoyed the finer things in life. Travel, clothes, good food. Almost dying because of believing in the wrong person?

That must have sucked.

Surely he understood that one woman was an anomaly? Having grown up in the pride, Stacey knew those kinds of incidences where they went nuts were rare. But he perhaps didn't know that. Perhaps she should tell him or, even better, show him that not all shifters were violent psychopaths. Bring him home to meet her family. Mama and Papa and all her siblings.

Hmm, then again, their chaos might send him running.

What am I doing? Thinking of introducing him to relatives. Hello, he was not boyfriend material. Casual sex, yes, but nothing more permanent. She had no interest in settling down and popping out babies. Unlike her sisters, she didn't get all gushy at the thought of children.

Children had dirty paw prints that left stains on clothes. They also expected constant care. Stacey wasn't into that. At all.

Most men, though, they wanted a family. A legacy to carry on their name. It made long-term relationships sour when they heard her philosophy on life.

Enjoy it.

Travel the world. Stay up late. But don't waste the day. Avoid the midday sun. Don't buy off a discount rack. And no babies.

Most of those men could handle but, for some reason, the last one really threw them off.

Best to stay single.

Staying single meant not caring about the fact that her ex-boyfriends moved on with a little Sally Homemaker.

Was Francois at this moment already moving on with Jan?

The very thought had her waving a waiter over with another drink.

By the time the adventuring party returned, she was sitting in the shade by the pool, sloshed and taking selfies that she posted and tagged her biatches in to make them jealous she was at a luxury resort while they were stuck at home. The riposte of texts back, most calling her jealous names, made her smile.

A massive shadow covered her slathered body. The tiny bikini meant there was a lot of skin that needed protection.

Stacey lifted her sunglasses to eye Francois properly. "You make a better door than a window," she observed.

"Is lying by the pool your idea of work?"

"You told me to stay out of jail. So I did."

His lip twitched. She was sure of it.

"I didn't think you'd listen."

"Your faith in me is astounding."

Yes, definitely some movement at the corner of his mouth.

"I have faith that you can find trouble wherever you are."

She didn't even try to contain her grin. "I do. It makes life interesting. You should try it sometime."

"Trouble is for thrill seekers."

"It is. And it is also for those who want to live life rather than play it safe."

"Taking chances can be deadly."

The subtle undercurrent to the words struck her.

"But only by taking a chance can you sometimes discover new and exciting things."

"Sometimes things die trying."

She held his gaze. "But what a way to go."

With a shake of his head, he severed the visual connection between them. "Every time you open your mouth, you give another reason why I should stay away from you."

"Liar. Every time I open my mouth, you wonder, will it fit? Does she spit or swallow?" The brazen words poured out of her, and she couldn't help but laugh as his expression got even more uptight.

With a hint of smoldering.

"Your mouth is filthy."

"I agree, I am soooooo dirty. Whatever will you do?" she purred. "Put me over your knee and spank me? We should probably go to our room for that."

"You should probably keep your voice down," he growled.

"Fuck 'em," she drawled, the alcohol making her bold. "We didn't share the same mother. It's allowed in some states." They also didn't share the same father, but his rebuke about keeping cover made her hold her tongue on that part.

"You're drunk."

"Yep." She held up her glass. The empty glass. "These are really fucking good." Made shifter-strong. Pound back a few and even she felt a buzz.

"How on earth did you manage to stay out of trouble today?" Francois said with a shake of his head.

"I was good." So good because he'd said he'd give her a prize.

"I doubt it."

His skepticism pissed her off and made her suspect something. "Are you trying to welch on our bet by calling me a liar?"

"I'm a man of my word. You'll get what I promised."

"Make it sound like a chore," she grumbled.

"More like disappointment."

"Because you don't want to smooch me." Her lips turned down.

He crouched by her chair and moved in close so only she could hear him.

"I want to kiss you. But why settle for a tame kiss? See, I'd assumed I'd return to you being incarcerated. Locked somewhere and in need of rescue. I had a plan to rescue you that would have rivaled something from the Wild West."

"You would have saved me?"

"Oh yes," he murmured, leaning close. "Saved you and then spanked your ass until it was pink and you couldn't sit for a few days."

She sucked in a breath. "Damn, sweetcheeks. You make me wish I'd given in to impulse today. Now that I know what you're planning, I'll try harder to get arrested next time."

He growled.

She chose to view it as a holy-shit-you're-hot kind of growl.

"You're impossible," he snapped, getting to his feet.

"Admit it, you like the challenge."

"If I want challenge, I'll play chess."

"Boring," she sang. But then because it was bothering her, she finally remarked on his disheveled appearance.

"Is it me, or do you look like you wrestled with the jungle and lost?" Dirt and other things streaked his shirt, and a scrape abraded his temple.

"A little mishap in the woods." Said with a false smile that didn't reach his eyes. "No big deal. I could, however, use a shower." He turned on his heel and walked away.

Since the view was mighty fine, she slid her glasses down on her nose and watched. It meant she got to see Jan scurry out from the clubhouse and make a beeline for the far side of the pool and engage in a conversation with Maurice.

Unfortunately, she couldn't make it out, but she noted how Maurice glanced at her then away quickly.

Children playing at subterfuge. How adorable. It made her wonder what had happened on the volcano tour.

And, hello, did Francois say he was showering? Code speak for join him? Either way, a naked hottie wasn't something she wanted to miss. Gathering her keg of sunscreen, she weaved her way back to their building, cursing its distance. Those mai tais were really good.

Despite the numerous debates to take a nap in some of the soft-looking grass along the way, she made it, and her bright yellow building came into sight. She noticed JF outside it talking to a girl. A girl with long red hair. *Who isn't me.*

The missing resort guest Shania had returned.

CHAPTER FOURTEEN

"HOLY SHIT, YOU FOUND SHANIA." Stacey sauntered close, and JF noticed how the woman shrank toward him, tucking into his frame for protection.

It caused Stacey to growl.

Interesting, did she see Shania as a threat? The woman looked rather unimposing he felt. She couldn't shift. She was slim, but not in any great physical shape. What did Stacey see that he didn't?

"I didn't exactly find her," Francois stated. "She just came wandering around the side of the building." Took him by surprise, given he was still kind of muddled on what had happened that afternoon.

I lost hours. From a supposed fall. Except that didn't seem right.

What happened? Last thing he remembered were eyes alit with malevolence racing at him from the jungle then weaving on the bench of the truck. Jan holding him against the cab so he didn't fall over.

The fuzzy spot in his mind meant he wasn't thinking clearly when Shania stepped into view.

"Where have you been?" Stacey asked, a hand on her hip and sounding quite demanding.

Yet it drew results.

Shania straightened. "What do you mean where? I've been on the resort."

"No you haven't. People have been looking for you."

"I was in the woods. Going for a walk." Shania tossed her head, her confidence returning fast.

"Pretty long freaking walk," Stacey stated.

"Why do people care if I went for a stroll? And how did anyone even miss me? I don't usually come out of my room until midafternoon."

JF noted the confusion and jumped in. "Ms. Korgunsen, do you realize you've been considered missing for more than three days?"

"No way. Stop screwing with me. So what if I went out last night and met a guy in the woods. I've hardly been gone days."

"Don't tell me you're believing the amnesia shtick," interjected Stacey with a snort. "She knows where she was. Don't even kid yourself. Look at her."

He did, noting the things that had bothered him but only now truly registered. Shania looked entirely too fresh and healthy. She'd obviously not wandered around in the jungle for days, or been kidnapped and abused by some psycho.

"So you admit to meeting a guy? Who was it? Someone on the resort?" Stacey hammered.

"I—" Shania's forehead knit into a frown. "I'm not sure of anything right now. My head is so fuzzy. The last thing I recall was running through the woods, enacting some fantasy the guy I was meeting had. But then there was a lion. Except he wasn't a lion."

"Was he a shifter?"

"You know about those?" Shania's eyes widened.

Given the woman was nose blind, he couldn't exactly condemn the fact that she didn't recognize what they were. He took on the role of good cop. Let Stacey do the bad cop. It was kind of hot when she got commanding.

Her jealousy was also cute, which was why he poked it. He put an arm around Shania. "You're safe talking with us. We know you're a dormant shifter. So you can tell us anything."

Stacey's eyes narrowed. "Was the person who took you a shifter?"

A roll of Shania's shoulders joined her admission. "He said he was a lion, but I can't really recognize someone by their scent."

"And scent may no longer apply," he muttered under his breath. Something about Shania's scent, more like the lack of one, bothered him. Shania smelled of soap and regular body odor. Nothing else.

No one else.

How did that happen if she'd spent a few days with him?

"Who was the man you were meeting?" Stacey asked.

"I shouldn't say. He works for the resort, and I don't want him getting in trouble."

"Even though he might have done something to you?" Stacey's voice pitched. "What the hell is wrong with you? We just finished telling you that you were missing for three days. Three fucking days." Stacey held up her fingers. "And you're worried about him getting fired? What part of he needs to be fired and arrested if he kidnapped you do you not get?"

"I wasn't kidnapped."

"Then say it," Stacey insisted. "Say, I was spending three days in bed with..." Stacey rolled a hand at Shania, encouraging her to say it.

Shania shook her head. "I'm sorry, but I don't think I want to talk to you. " She put a hand to her head. "Everything is so cloudy."

"Ms. Korgunsen." Jan shouted her name sharply as she came marching down the cultured path. "Thank goodness you're back." Someone had obviously been watching the security cameras scattered around the resort to have remarked it so quickly. "We were ever so worried about you."

"I think I'm going to gag if she gets any sweeter," Stacey murmured.

"Have I really been gone for days?" Shania asked. "I can't remember anything."

"Someone had too much fun," teased Jan, wrapping an arm around Shania. "Why don't we go and get you something to eat. Maybe a bit of food and drink will help you recall your adventure."

"She needs to see a doctor," Stacey stated.

"We'll have her checked out. Never fear. Our resort doctor is the best."

"Maybe I should come along. For moral support," Stacey offered.

Francois almost snickered as Stacey poured on the fake sincerity.

"You want to show support for a woman you barely know?" Jan blinked at Stacey, who smiled.

"All women should stand together in times of need." Folding her hands over her belly, Stacey attempted to appear benign.

"Don't worry. I'll make sure we take good care of Shania and figure out what happened. Those pesky jungle bugs can do all kinds of things to a body." Spoken with a giggle as Jan led Shania off.

"Jungle bug my ass," Stacey muttered as she took a few steps to follow.

JF grabbed her by the arm to halt her. "Where are you going?"

"After them." She tugged at his grip. "I have more questions."

"They're not going to let you in there to speak with Shania. You're a guest, remember?" he muttered.

"Maybe it's time I tell them I'm here under Arik's authority."

"You'll blow our cover." As if she'd not already done that on the patio. Either people would clue in or really wonder at their relationship.

"If I don't go, then how else do you suggest I question Shania?"

"Forget her for now. Question her later when she's released. I have a better plan."

"And you want me included in on it?" She sounded so surprised.

"I need you—"

Say it. Say you can't stop thinking of her. If you don't sink balls deep inside, your balls will probably fall off.

Instead, he ignored his more passionate beast to say, "—to come with me and visit that volcano. Tonight."

She didn't exclaim in excitement. Rather her nose wrinkled. "Why would we go mucking around a dead volcano at night when we have a comfortable bed here?"

Oh, the things that made him imagine...

"You'd take sleeping in a bed over adventure? Who are you, and what did you do with my crazy princess?" Wasn't she the one craving adventure all the time?

"It's because I am a princess that I'm suggesting we get naked in a bed instead of tromping around in a jungle at night. Do you have any idea how many insects there are out there?"

"I'll offer up my body instead to them."

"Is this your way of saying you're sweeter tasting than me?"

"I doubt anything tastes sweeter than you." The words escaped him, and he wished someone would punch him.

What the fuck was that garbage I just driveled?

The truth.

"You say something panty wetting like that and you wonder why I think we should hit the bed."

"I can't believe you'd ditch our mission for sex." Then again, he kind of felt the same way. He wanted to ditch a whole bunch of other stuff, like responsibility and his pants.

"Not just any sex. Good sex. And what mission are you talking about?"

Did she really already forget? "The one that just walked off."

"You mean the woman who probably spent the last few days giving her lungs and pussy a workout?"

"You're assuming she went on a tryst. She doesn't remember anything."

"So she claims. Or maybe she doesn't want to say."

"I don't think she's lying," he said as he led the way upstairs to their rooms.

"Neither do I, but anything else makes no sense. Explain how Shania can disappear for days and return not recalling anything, except a vague recollection of running through the woods."

"I can't."

"Because it's impossible unless she was taken by aliens." She whirled around, her eyes wide.

"Don't even say it," he cautioned.

"But—"

He held up his finger to shush her. "Aliens did not kidnap her."

She deflated. "Spoilsport. It would have been a cool explanation."

"I'd rather a correct explanation. Maybe Shania will get a medical examination and they'll find something."

"Like what? From what I saw, the woman bore no signs of bruising or scratches. No evidence of malnutrition. She's returned, it seems, in the same condition she left but with no memories."

"Could be a drug." Perhaps the same one that caused him to forget a swath of time that afternoon.

"A drug to make her forget fabulous nookie? Now you're talking crazy, sweetcheeks."

"Maybe the sex wasn't memorable," he noted.

"Which obviously rules you out as a suspect." She winked at him. "I doubt there's any forgetting you."

"Why would you even think of me as a suspect? I arrived at this island with you."

"Or did you come here vacationing, a few days at a time, kidnap women for wild sex, then ditch them with no memories, saving them from the trauma of never riding your big dick again?"

"You look like a lady." He eyed her up and down, the silken wrap tied sarong style around her body. Her bare shoulders elegant and inviting. "Sometimes even talk like a lady. And then you say the most filthy things."

"Only filthy because of how I look. I bet there's some of my biatches that you wouldn't even bat an eye at if they said it."

"Are you suggesting I spend time with another woman to see if your theory is true?" He baited her jealous side.

She reacted by straightening. Her gaze narrowed. "I see what you're doing, sweetcheeks. Trying to get me off track. But here's the thing. A lioness can always multi-task. Say like Luna, a few years ago, was in a drinking contest in some bar down in Texas and some dude tried to grab her boob as she was doing shots. She broke his hand and still managed to win that bet. I lost a precious pair of cowboy boots that day, but I learned a lesson."

He knew he shouldn't, but he asked, "What lesson?"

"Don't get in a drinking match with Luna."

Arriving at her door, as she held her arm up to let them in, he made sure to slide in front of her to enter first.

"If they wanted me, they would have struck this afternoon while you gone," she noted, shoving past him into the room. "And I highly doubt whoever took and released Shania would grab someone else so soon."

"Was that logic I heard, princess?"

She smirked at him. "I'm not all just good looks, sweetcheeks."

"So use those smarts and tell me what you think happened to Shania."

"I'd say this is a case of Occam's Razor."

"And what do you think the most plausible explanation is?"

"I say she's lying. For all we know, she spent a couple of days with a married man who doesn't want his wife to know."

"Is this speculation based on any sort of fact?" He snapped his fingers. "Did you perhaps crack her phone?"

"What phone?"

"The one you filched from her room."

"Yeah, about that." Stacey stepped out of her sandals as she paused. "That phone was kind of stolen from my room the first night we went to dinner."

His face hardened. "What do you mean it's gone? Someone entered your room and stole something and you didn't think to tell me?"

"Telling you means I would have gotten a lecture. And it wasn't as if I could tell management that the phone I borrowed was stolen."

He crossed his arms, scowled, but managed to not tap his foot. "These are things I need to know, princess."

"I'm telling you now, aren't I?"

He glared.

It did not make her repent at all.

Stacey slid off her robe and hit the bathroom to run

the shower. He would have left, but she kept talking to him.

"We need to talk about Shania and the married guy who drugged her for sex," she shouted, having left the door open.

"Again, you don't know for sure what happened to her."

She popped back out, her body exposed in her tiny bikini. "I gave you a very plausible theory. What's yours? I can tell you what she wasn't. She wasn't sold to the black market. " Stacey ticked off fingers. "Wasn't beaten or abused. No body parts appeared missing. Why kidnap her at all?"

"That's what we need to find out, and I think we'll find those answers at the volcano." Find out what happened to him during his blackout.

"What makes you think a volcano has any kind of answers? Did you find something?" The adventurer in her perked up "Ancient temple? Graveyard of bones?"

"Gum wrapper."

She blinked. "Are you trying to tell me that, on the basis of some litter, you want to go trekking around in the dark? Did something bite you in the woods today?"

For some reason, his hand went to his neck. "They breed them big out here."

"Exactly, and yet you want to send my succulent body into their lair when the mosquitoes are most active." She shook her head. "You do realize the bar is serving fish-bowl-sized margaritas tonight. I could use a few, especially since *you*"—pointed stare—"refuse to give me any."

145

He wanted to give it to her all too much. That was the real problem.

He veered his mind away from that dangerous corner. "There was more than just the wrapper out there. Something is going on around that volcano. You should have smelled it."

"How could you smell anything over Jan's perfume?"

A good point given Jan's aroma irritated the membrane in his nose and chafed on his last nerve.

"This isn't about Jan. Ignore her."

"Why should I since you didn't?"

"Are you seriously going to have a jealous fit now?" Because it was totally sexy when she did it.

He shouldn't like it. Seriously. The last thing he needed was a jealous lioness fucking shit up.

But when Stacey did it...

"This is not jealousy." Her lower lip pouted.

It totally was.

For some reason, it made him admit, "I have no interest in Jan."

"Yet you come back smelling of her. The stench of it is offensive." She sniffed and tossed her head, sending her hair rippling.

"Would you stop whining if I said I'd rather wear your scent?"

The words took a moment to filter. When they did, she smiled. Sunshine of fucking epic proportions emerged that slayed him where he stood.

"Actually, I would feel better if you wore my scent. Thanks for offering." Then she launched herself at him.

More than instinct, but a need to hold her meant he caught her, held her with ease.

"Are you seriously doing that?" he asked as she rubbed her cheek against his.

"I am. You said I could mark you with my scent. So shut up for a second while I finish."

"This is why I don't get involved with cats or other pets," he growled.

"Admit it, you are totally dying to stroke me and make me purr."

"Lions don't purr."

"Are you sure about that? Maybe you should give it a try."

He wanted to. "We don't have time for this, princess."

With a sigh, she unwound herself from him, and the smug smile announced how happy she was that she'd won again.

He wore her scent. At her sudden frown, he made the mistake of asking, "What's wrong?"

"It occurs to me that you've not stripped us both naked and rubbed your essence all over me."

"If a woman is mine, she doesn't need my smell to know." He turned from her and headed for the partition leading to his room.

"Must we go to the volcano tonight?"

"Yes. Because the gum wrapper and smell thing aren't the only things wonky about that place. I lost time." He admitted it to her, knowing it would distract her from the heat sizzling between them.

Except she misunderstood. "Yeah, you lost time going on that stupid trip. Instead of hanging around here helping me find out who might know something about Shania's disappearance."

"No, I mean I lost time, as in one minute I was facing down a charging boar—"

"Did you bring some back to share? Wild game is the best."

"No, because I passed out."

She blinked. "Excuse me. Did you say passed out? Was it that big and scary?"

"No. I passed out because something bit me."

"I knew those jungle bugs were vicious."

"I don't think it was a bug. Something got me here." He pointed to his neck. "And here." He pointed to his ass.

She leaned closer to take a look at the skin. "I don't see anything on your neck. Drop your pants and bend over so I can peek at your butt."

Brazen command that he would not obey. "There's nothing to see. Anything that pricked me would have healed by now."

"What was it do you think? Spider? Mosquito? Alien sporting a needle-like appendage?"

"Dart."

"Hold on a second. You think someone darted you? And you passed out?" She sounded incredulous.

"Yeah. I'm not too impressed either. It must have been something new on the market because I'm usually more resistant to shit."

She shook her head. "Is this how you're going to excuse whatever you did with Jan this afternoon? Adopt Shania's lame story and use it as your cover instead of telling me the truth?"

Exactly how had her mind veered back to Jan? "This is the truth."

"According to you. Why should I believe a word you say?"

"Why would I lie?"

"I don't know. You seem to think I might be yanking your chain because some chick a long time ago screwed you over."

"She tried to kill me."

"Cry me a river. Do you know how many people have tried to kill me? It's not easy being this beautiful." She flicked her hair.

His lip twitched. "I see what you're doing." He did. She was trying to prove that they could only take each other at face value.

"What? Showing you what a moron you are? Gee, that wasn't too hard. The fact is, sweetcheeks, you got a bum rap from a crazy broad. I can see you might be gun-shy, but at one point, you know, I know you know, that not all of us, hell, not even most of us, are psychopathic killers."

"I don't know. I've met the pride ladies, and more than a few are a few crayons short of a full box."

"It's part of our charm, but it doesn't make us untrustworthy. You gotta let go of your fear."

"I am not scared." He couldn't help but straighten with pique.

"Aren't you?" She took a step closer. His body quivered, slightly leaning back. "I'm not going to hurt you."

"What if I'm concerned about the hurt going the other way?" Stacey was a force of nature. Get too close and he risked getting swept away.

"You think you could hurt me?" She laughed. "That's cute, sweetcheeks."

"You don't understand what lurks within me. The monster I hide." The beast that pulsed and begged for another taste.

"You're no more a monster than I am. You should see me when I'm PMS-ing and someone eats my last piece of chocolate."

He gave her a stern stare.

Clearly she had been the recipient of many a stern stare in her life, as it had no effect.

"This is not a joking matter," he grumbled.

"You are much too serious. Lighten up. Not everything is doom and gloom."

"You're impossible to talk to. And we've gotten way off track. Are you in or out with the volcano?" In or out. In or out. Fuck, he wanted in and out.

"Totally in, if you promise to squish any bugs we come across."

"I'll kill them." Anything that threatened her. "And what will you do for me?"

"Look pretty while you do it?" She grinned.

JF shook his head and sighed. "I'm a fucking moron for even contemplating bringing you along."

"Why are you? Why didn't you just go without telling me?" She cocked her head, waiting for a reply.

"Because you might come across as a flake, but I know you're good in a fight."

"And how do you know that?"

"I've seen the lionesses in battle."

"I'm better than them," she confided. "Just so you know."

Much better or he would have never taken notice of

her. "We'll have to wait until nightfall so we're harder to see."

"Oh dear, whatever shall we do in the meantime?" She fluttered her lashes.

He knew that look.

Wanted to explore it. Being stupidly stubborn, he turned away, saying, "I'll collect us some things we might need and order in some room service."

He wasn't expecting the shoe she whipped at his head. He froze but didn't turn around, so she tossed her other sandal and hit him in the ass.

That got his attention.

Whipping around, he didn't say a word, just strode back to her, grabbing her by the upper arms and snapping, "Why must you keep antagonizing me?"

"Because."

"Because is not an answer," he roared. "Why must you vex me?"

"Because it's fun."

"Maybe for you. But you're driving me insane." He huffed, every inch of him taut with tension.

The beast inside pulsed.

Take her. Claim her.

He fought back against the beast.

She poked it.

CHAPTER FIFTEEN

"ABOUT TIME YOU WENT A LITTLE CRAZY," she said, running a finger down his chest, tracing the seam for his buttons.

"You don't know what you're doing."

"I'm unleashing your passion, sweetcheeks." A passion she wanted.

"My passion might kill you."

"A whole bunch of things could kill me. If it's meant to happen during sex, toe-curling sex I might add, then so be it."

"Did you ever think that maybe I totally suck at it?"

Such a blatant lie. The man was sex on a stick, and she wanted a lick.

She laughed. "The way you make me feel, you could probably just blow on my pussy and I'd come."

A ripple went through him, and he turned away. "Leave me alone."

"Are you afraid to have sex?"

"Not usually." A grudging admission.

"So you think sex with me is going to make you snap? Do you have any idea how hot that is, sweetcheeks?" She grabbed him by the shirt to tug him close. "Don't worry. I'm going to help you stop being afraid."

"How?"

"By having wildly satisfying, toe-curling, scream-inducing sex." Brazen, but then again, subtle wouldn't work with him. The man appeared utterly determined to close himself off. Too bad, because she wanted in.

"A woman shouldn't ask for sex."

"You're right. I shouldn't have to, and yet I am because I am dealing with the most stubborn man alive. We need this, sweetcheeks." She tilted her head and craned on tiptoe enough to nip at his chin. "We're both wound so tight that we'll be no good in the field. Think of it as stress relief. Use me to satisfy your needs."

"Some of my needs are dark and dangerous."

"I know, and I think the fact you're afraid you'll lose control with me on account I'm so wonderfully awesome is the sexiest thing ever."

There went that lovely tic of his. "I can control myself."

"Prove it."

"You won't stop, will you?"

"Not until you make me come so hard I see stars."

With a groan, he finally succumbed.

Reeled her into his arms and dipped his head to claim her lips, branding her with the force behind his embrace. The hunger in him couldn't be hidden, and her own arousal refused to be ignored. He coaxed her mouth open, teasing her bottom lip between his, melting her from the inside out.

With need pulsing in her, she leaned into him, pressed into his hardness. Her arms wrapped around him, clasping him tight, loving the solid strength of him.

His lips pressed hard against hers, a forceful branding that she reciprocated. A part of her, a large noisy part, wanted to claim this male, to imprint her essence on him for all to see.

The world needs to see that he's mine. The possessive feeling only grew the more she got to know him.

Given she finally had him where she wanted him, she couldn't help but stroke his body as they kissed, her hands skimming over the fabric of his shirt, exploring his hard ridges, cupping his firm ass.

She slid her hands past his waistband to cup his cheeks. She dug her nails in, and he growled at her. So sexy. She squeezed him and growled back. The sound did something to him. Unleashed a new level of urgency and wildness.

Hoisting her changed the angle of their embrace. She no longer had to crane to kiss him, a good thing because he'd rendered her legs quite useless. Fire consumed her, igniting all her nerves, burning her up from the inside out. And she hungered for more.

He slipped a wet tongue into her open mouth to rub against hers, and she sucked it, finally truly tasting him. Craving him more than any chocolate she'd ever had.

The layers of clothes keeping their bodies separated irritated. Didn't the fabric realize this moment deserved nakedness?

Already having hoisted her into the air, it was easy for him to walk until her back hit a wall, partially supporting her and giving him the ability to grind his pelvis against hers. Rock hard meet soft and wet. He rubbed, and she moaned, the friction delicious.

"Strip me," she whispered. "I want to feel your skin against mine." She could feel Francois fighting for control. Didn't he understand she wanted him wild? She could handle it. Handle the passion he tried to keep buried.

Her lithe thighs wrapped around his waist, keeping him locked against her body. Her bikini bottoms chafed against her sensitive flesh.

He must have read her mind because he solved that problem, a tug of his fingers ripping the seam, turning her bottoms into scrap fabric. He tugged it free and tossed it to the side. Revealing her, staring at her with hunger in his eyes.

With her back still pressed against the wall, he ran his fingers down her lower belly, teased the short pelt covering her mound before dipping lower, causing her to moan.

"You're wet." Stated in a gruff voice.

Like duh. She'd been wet from the moment she met him.

"Taste me." She totally wanted to feel his mouth on her, lapping at her cream. She let her legs loose from his waist and planted them on tiptoe on the floor. "Get on your knees. Worship me."

He groaned.

"Don't make me wait. Lick me. Now." An imperial command, and yet he muttered, "As the princess wishes," as he slid down, somehow keeping her upright as he went to this knees.

He nudged himself between her legs, pushing them

over his shoulders, supporting her so that she didn't fall and bringing his mouth in line with her sex. He blew on it, cold breath against her moist core.

Her turn to groan. "Don't tease me."

"I'll do whatever I fucking please with you," he growled.

The words caused a shiver. No denying the hunger in them. The possessiveness.

A flick of his tongue against her nether lips had her crying out. He licked her again, over and over, hot teases of his tongue on her flesh, parting her that he might lap at her honey.

She clutched at his head, not wanting him to move. It felt so good. So deliciously erotic. He found her clit and worked it, pulling at it with his lips, teasing it with his tongue. Lashing it so that she throbbed with need.

"Fuck me," she said in a low murmur. "I want to feel you inside me when I come."

"But I want you to come on my tongue," he replied against her sex, the vibration of his words a tease of its own.

He then proceeded to truly lick her. Pushing his tongue against her, nipping at her clit. Truly making her crazy, so crazy she came, a sharp scream erupting from her as he drew a climax from her flesh.

"Now I'll fuck you," he growled before rising. Holding her aloft with one strong arm, he used the other to undo the fly of his jeans. His cock sprang forward and slapped her wet, throbbing flesh.

The jerk teased her, rubbing the fat head of his dick against her wet slit.

"Now," she demanded, leaning forward to nip at his lower lip.

"I'll fuck you when I'm damned well ready, woman."

He teased her some more, rubbing her sensitized clit, bringing back that panting edge of passion that had her moaning and squirming against him.

Without warning, he suddenly slid into her snug sheath, and she cried out as he filled her. Filled her and stretched her in all the right ways.

Wanting to keep him close, she gripped him tightly with her arms and legs. He pistoned her, hips pulling back and then slamming, back and then slamming. The movement meant she couldn't maintain a kiss with him so she contented herself with sucking and biting the skin at his neck.

"If you don't stop..." He didn't finish the sentence, but she knew he was close, close to losing control.

Good.

She nipped him, and Francois's head snapped back. The cords in his neck bulged, and she licked them, licked even as she tightened her body around him. With her back pressed against the wall, his hands cupping her ass cheeks, he pumped her. Pumped her hard and fast, slamming his cock in and out of her, drawing mewling cries.

Her flesh, so recently sated, ignited again, her second climax teetering. He changed his angle, and a sharp cry left her as his new stroke found her G-spot over and over. Bumped it. Ground it. Her fingers clawed at his back.

It was too much. She came again, convulsing and screaming, her flesh pulsing around his cock.

And his body tensed, and when his mouth found the curve of her neck and shoulder, he uttered a mighty sound against her skin, the sharp tips of teeth pinched, but she didn't care as his body thrust one last time. Buried deep. Pulsing. Marking her finally with his seed.

She felt him sucking at her neck, the skin slightly bruised but not broken. He pulled away with a groan.

She slapped a hand on his lips before he could speak. "If you say we shouldn't have done that, I'll nut punch you."

"That's not very ladylike," he mumbled behind her fingers.

"Haven't you figured out yet that I'm only a lady in public?" She smiled.

He took that smile and turned it into astonishment. "You should try being a lady in private sometime. A man likes a challenge."

"Is this your not-so-subtle way of getting me to change so I don't throw myself at you?"

"This is my not-so-subtle way of making you seem unattainable so I have the enjoyment of seducing you."

"You want to seduce me?" The very fact that he said it was a seduction in and of itself.

He dragged her close, his lips almost touching hers. "I want to do so many things to your body. Things that would make you scream. Decadent pleasures that would have you scratching my back."

"Didn't that just happen?"

"Imagine it even more intensely."

"How about you show me?"

"No. We don't have time." Whispered onto her lips before he set her apart from him.

Was he seriously about to walk away? "Get back over here," she demanded.

"Nightfall approaches. Ready to go?" he asked.

"Not really." Her pussy grumbled that he was a tease. A part of her hummed with excitement because he'd all but admitted he was besotted with her. And yet he still wanted to go play Tarzan in the jungle.

"If you want to stay here, go ahead. But I'm going back to the volcano."

"I'm coming." Not in an erotic way, but she wouldn't let him go alone. "But don't expect me to enjoy it. You're not the one who's got to run through the jungle watching for traps."

"Who said anything about running, princess? What if I said we could fly?"

"How? Did you rent a helicopter?"

"Why the fuck would I do that? I don't have wings for show."

"In case you hadn't noticed, I don't have any."

"I'll carry you."

Her expression brightened. "Carry me?"

Containing her glee proved hard, which was why their departure was delayed. She threw herself at him and rode him like a cowgirl going after a first place ribbon. Then there was more time wasted as they sluiced off. During that soapy exploration, he explained a few rules.

"Rule number one. No getting in the way of my wings unless you want to go splat."

"Does this mean I don't get to ride your back dragon style? But what if I want to channel my inner Daenerys?"

"I have no idea what that means, but I'm pretty sure whatever it is will be a no. I will carry you, or you can walk. Which leads to rule number two. No distracting me."

"Who me?" She pointed at herself and tried to look innocent. Tried so hard and yet she failed.

Crossing his arms first, he presented her with a stern look. "Yes, you. No kissing, licking, stroking, or piercing shrieks while flying."

"So just to be clear, does this mean no aerial 69s?"

"Um." For a moment he went cross-eyed. She allowed it. After all, she knew what he was thinking about, his semi-erection poking at her in the shower. The length covered in soap suds proclaimed where his mind went. "No. This is what I mean about distracting," he said, shaking himself free from whatever fantasy shook him.

"Well, that's no fun. Does this mean we'll never do some hanky-panky among the clouds?"

"Princess, this is not the time for that discussion."

"Fine. But I will note that if I somehow accidentally end up with my crotch in your face and your cock in my mouth, it will be your fault for not talking it out further with me when you had a chance. Have I mentioned just how orally talented I am?"

The proclamation delayed them another five minutes in the shower because the man had some damned stamina.

In order to ensure no further distractions after that, he banned Stacey to her room. "Don't come back until you're wearing some damned clothes, woman."

Since her body finally seemed sated for the moment, she allowed him his command. Besides, she finally had the perfect opportunity to wear her specially crafted outfit made for a jungle trek.

His eyes just about popped out of his head when he saw it and asked, "What the fuck are you wearing?"

She spun to show off her ensemble. "Do you like it? I had it modified from the original design so that it would accommodate me better if I had to shift."

"It's a fucking superhero costume."

It sure was. Tights, body suit, skintight of course to show off her curves. The giant G on the front, for Gorgeous, glittered. She'd opted for the short cape despite *The Incredibles* showing the dangers of having one. She'd make sure to steer clear of any plane engines.

"Don't be jealous, sweetcheeks. When we get back home, I'll have a suit custom made for you as my sidekick."

His brows rose. "Oh hell no, princess. I am not your sidekick. And I don't want a costume." He crossed his arms.

"Good point. A costume would just hide that delicious bod." It occurred to her that if he went around half naked then other biatches would get an eyeful. She knew how to fix that. Turn a profit by buying some stock in an eye patch company.

"Take off that ridiculous outfit."

"You want me naked again? If you insist, sweetcheeks." As she went peel off her clothes, he groaned.

"Stop. Keep it on."

"Keep it on, take it off. Make up your mind," she grumbled, but she was secretly pleased it got to stay. She'd had her superhero suit enhanced since the graveyard zombie fight. The costume now had stretchier fabric with a special flap at the back for a tail. It meant she could shift without losing her clothes, and even better, if she shifted back, the material would shrink too, leaving her clothed instead of naked. Thank you, fellows at the secret lab that could not be named.

"Come here." He pointed to a spot in front of him.

She allowed the command and stood close.

Swept into his arms, she only had time to bite her tongue so she wouldn't exclaim "Whee" before he ran for the open sliding glass doors. With a single bound, he hit the lip of the balcony and a moment later soared into the air.

It was freaking amazing, which was why she had her camera out to take pictures.

"What are you doing?" No surprise he didn't sound very happy. Probably because they hadn't had sex in like the last ten minutes.

"Taking pics for my biatches back home. Smile." He grimaced, which worked too. She tagged the image before posting it. #suckitbiatches #timeofmylife.

"What happened to no distractions?"

"I turned off the flash."

A big sigh escaped him.

She grinned as she tucked the phone into the pouch on her sleeve. She then wound her arms around his neck to enjoy the ride.

This time of night, and with the sky overcast, there wasn't much to see. The jungle they flew over didn't have any lights shining, nothing but shadows nestled upon shadows. It made her wonder how he could find their path.

"Can you see in the dark?"

"Not exactly."

"How can you be sure we're not lost?" she asked.

"I know where we're going."

"How?"

"I just do."

Having watched her fair share of documentaries, she exclaimed, "You've got bat radar, don't you?"

That earned her another sigh.

If she managed one more, she'd have a hat trick.

Or he'd drop her.

That wouldn't stop her from trying.

All too soon, because she rather enjoyed flying through the sky, he landed and announced, "We're here."

"I left an air-conditioned room, comfortable bed, and stocked mini bar for this?" This being the bottom of a mountain and shrubs. Lots of thorny shrubs.

"Find a clue and you won't need a bed to get a prize."

"Just to clarify, are we talking about sex?"

"Yes."

"Together?" Again, she'd learned to always make sure of the details.

"Yes, together. Unless you'd prefer someone else?" His fangs flashed as he snarled.

The jealousy was cute. "No worries, sweetcheeks. You're the only man I want to get wild with." She trailed a finger down his bare chest, loving the strange texture of his other skin.

"No distractions. Find something good and I'll give you whatever you need."

"Anything?" The very thought excited.

"Yes." The word rumbled, low and sexy.

With that kind of incentive, she leaped from his arms and whipped out a glow stick. A crack and shake later, they had green light.

"Where did you get that?" he asked.

"I told you this suit was awesome. All kinds of hidden surprises. Wanna see?"

"Stay focused."

She was focused. On getting him to remove his pants. Now that he'd shifted back, his frame slightly less bulky, the loose shorts hung low on his lean hips.

Snap. Snap. The fingers clicking had her gaze rising. "While your obsession with my dick is flattering, we are here on business."

Right. What the heck was wrong with her? He was right. She needed to act more ladylike instead of drooling constantly around him. "What am I looking for?"

"I'm not sure, but this is the spot I lost consciousness." He knelt down on the ground, fingers brushing the soil.

"Because you were drugged." It still made her snicker.

"You can stop saying it in that tone. I know what happened. Or didn't happen. One moment I was facing off with a boar, and then..." He trailed off. Shrugged and looked off into the shadows as he said, "I woke up in the back of the truck with Jan claiming I fell and knocked myself out."

"I still can't believe you fell for that obvious lie? I mean, seriously, I've seen you move; you're not clumsy."

"I know I'm not, which is why I think it was a drug."

"Probably the bug that wasn't a bug that bit you."

"Two bites that I remember. Then I supposedly fell,

which probably explains my temple." He raised his fingers to the healing scrape. "When I woke up, I recall feeling disoriented and lightheaded."

"Why am I just hearing about the lightheadedness now?"

"Because you never shut up long enough for me to get a word in edgewise."

"Then you should talk faster." Or use his mouth for other things. "Now I know you keep insisting you got Mickey'd, but is it possible you just fainted from the heat?"

"I did not faint." Said with utter disdain.

"Technically, you did. What else do you call face planting?"

"You are really making me regret the choice of bringing you." He kept running his fingers over the ground as if he could find something by feel.

"Oh please, you and I both know that having me along is like having your own personal pocket of sunshine."

"I hate the sun."

"What a coincidence, so do I."

"Bullshit. I know you like to sunbathe," he retorted.

"Behind a strong UV filter. I burn unless slathered in vampire-proof lotion."

"So why volunteer to come to the tropics?"

"Because, hello, have you seen this body in a bikini?"

His lips tilted just a little. "It would be a shame to hide it from the world."

"Well ,that's a rude thing to say." She planted her hands on her hips.

"I just said you looked good."

"And then had no problem with me showing it off. Whereas I would keep you swaddled so nobody could see your sexy bod."

"Would you feel better if I said I'd drain the life out of any man who eyes you with lust?"

"Yes." Talk about super romantic.

"Won't happen. I am not a jealous killer."

Super letdown. "That's no fun. You know, Teena's husband, Dmitri, does insanely wicked things to those who stare overly long at his wife."

"You're not my wife."

"Yet."

He glared.

She clapped her hands. "There you go. That's the look I want to see you use when you're jealous. Followed by a vicious mauling."

"Did it ever occur to you that I do something better than killing?"

"Like what?"

"The best revenge against other guys is to take you into my arms." He drew her near. "And kiss you deeply, showing ownership."

"Yes," she whispered.

"Then slapping you on the ass and telling you to fetch me a beer." He smacked her butt.

"How is that supposed to make them jealous?"

"If you were a man, you'd understand." Turning from her, Francois moved off, his gaze intent on the ground.

She smiled. He was totally coming around. Not long now before he finally admitted he couldn't imagine living without her—and he fetched her chocolate. Beer indeed. He'd soon learn.

"What are we looking for?" she asked, crouching down.

"I'm not sure. But I'll know it if I find it."

"Are we still looking for that damned gum wrapper?"

"No. That was just a clue that the place I stumbled on had seen traffic. When I fell, I thought I saw something."

"A ghost?"

"No."

"Jan's boobs?"

"No," said on a note that said his cheek had that tic again.

"Good thing. I'd have to kill her if she'd flashed them."

"Let's try and stay on track here, princess."

"Perhaps instead of playing a guessing game, you should tell me what you saw."

"Maybe if you shut your mouth, woman, for more than five seconds, I could tell you."

"If you're going to beat around the bush, then I'm going to jump in. If you don't like it, gag me. I know you've got something just the right size to do that."

"You're impossible."

"And sexy."

"Very," he growled. "Which is I should have left you at the resort."

"But then we wouldn't be having a blast out in the middle of nowhere."

Sigh.

Fist pump. She had her hat trick.

"Hey, sweetcheeks, is it me, or do I smell chicken."

"Isn't the expression fish? And I thought you bathed."

Why did he always have to make the most awesome jokes at the wrong times? She punched him in the arm. "You'd better mean fish in a delicious sushi kind of way. But, seriously, I smell something cooking."

He frowned, his features taking on a devilish cast in the glowing light of her stick. He inhaled deep. "Hot damn, I smell it too."

"Could it be someone camping out here?" she asked.

"Doubtful. While they allow some small daytime treks, according to them, no overnights are allowed. Definitely no fires. The boar my group hunted down was skinned out here but brought back to the resort for cooking."

"So someone is breaking the rules." Rule-breaking plus a lioness in a special-order suit equaled a good time about to happen.

He sounded thoughtful as he stood and stared up the mountain. "If there is someone living out here, then they could perhaps be the person who stole Shania and wiped her memories."

And even if they weren't, this cat had to know. "Let's invite ourselves to dinner."

Treading quietly, she made a mental note to modify her costume, given her Lycra slippers with their slim rubber did not provide much protection against the sharp rocks on the ground.

"I should have worn my heels," she grumbled.

"Can't run in heels," he remarked.

"Says a man. I can run just fine in them. I'm the pride champion."

"I would have thought it was talking the most without taking a breath."

"No, that belongs to Melly. Biatch has incredible lungs."

"I think you need a rematch."

She jumped up and pecked him on the cheek. "Aren't you just sweet. And I know exactly how to practice. You'll have to time me when I'm giving you head."

He stumbled.

She flicked her hair and followed her nose. In the process, they stumbled along a scantily used path comprised of bent blades of scraggly grass and wilting leaves that had been brushed aside one too many times. But other than a few expected smells, rodents, wild boar, even a goat, there was nothing sentient. No shifter, no human. Yet, it wasn't an animal who'd made the path and dropped the sandwich wrapper.

As the scent of food grew stronger, they found themselves at the base of the volcano, the lumpy surface of it rising. The smell wafted down on them from above, the volcano not quite as steep here, but still challenging enough.

"Guess we're climbing," he noted. He'd reverted back to his hybrid shape for the hunt, and whilst he seemed more animalistic than man, he spoke perfectly fine. Looked mighty fine, too, even if he wasn't a lion.

The only thing he wore was a pair of dark shorts. As they climbed, his taut butt moving ahead of her, she imagined them bedazzled with a giant F on the ass. Francois the Ferocious. It had a nice ring. She wondered if he'd be open to a cape. Then again, he did have those awesome wings.

Something buzzed close by her cheek. The damned

insects had found them, and they showed no respect for this lioness on a mission. Biting her indeed.

As if that wasn't irritating enough, the damp air made her perspire. Lovely. Nothing said hot seductress more than stanky pits.

Then her nails, the beautifully French manicured nails, broke on the rough rocks. She could have sobbed. Now how would she rake them down Francois's back later in bed?

Complaining wasn't an option. Not when the mystery thickened and the smell of food cooking got stronger. The aroma appeared to waft from a cave, the opening of it boasting a wide ledge swept free of debris. Having reached it first, Francois turned around and offered her a hand, the first one since they started the climb. A man who respected her as an equal, but could still show some courtesy.

Did they have time for a quickie?

"Do you smell anything?" he asked. Was this a hint that he noticed her wet panties? "Human, or shifter?"

Trust him to stay focused. She held in a sigh and inhaled. Then sniffed again. She shook her head. "Other than some yummy stew, I don't smell anything at all."

Which didn't seem right. A clear path rose up the mountain. She could see the disturbance as they climbed, even found a tuft of fabric caught on a jagged edge. But not a single scent.

"Could it be a whampyr?" she asked. "Most of you don't smell."

"What do you mean most? We don't at all. You can't smell us unless we choose to wear a scent."

False. Perhaps at first she couldn't read his flavor, but

now that they'd been intimate, the musk of him, a very subtle essence unlike any she'd ever scented, marked him.

"You didn't answer the question. Could it be a whampyr?"

"I don't think so. We can usually recognize our own kind." He frowned. "And we are not solitary creatures. We tend to congregate in colonies."

"How do we know there's not a colony in that mountain?"

"Because."

"What do you mean because?"

"There is no proper food source here."

"The jungle is full of life."

"We can't survive on animals alone, and the population here is too sparse to feed on without notice."

"How do you eat at home? Do you like go hunting for crooks and stuff and suck them dry? Raid blood banks?"

"We don't do things that will have us noticed. Gaston provides."

"What if he didn't?"

"Then we would adapt."

"Rumor has it that the whampyrs that revolted against Gaston had a thing for shifter blood."

"It is true that your life's essence is rather sweet to us. But it is also forbidden. The treaties between shifters and whampyr are old. It is why Gaston could show no mercy to those who betrayed him."

"Does this mean you could be in big doo-doo if someone found out you nipped me?" If that was the case, she'd have to be careful not to tattle too much about their sexual exploits.

"The rule has some flexibility. If a whampyr and a

shifter become unlikely allies or lovers, then some exchange of fluids is expected and allowed. So long as it is mutual."

"In other words, we can totally become a couple."

"That's not what I said."

She blew a raspberry. "Give it up, sweetcheeks. You have no excuse to avoid me."

"On the contrary, I have a long list of reasons to avoid you."

"But you won't. Because you like me."

"Who said I liked you?"

"Do you really want me to force you to prove it out here on a ledge to the tantalizing smell of soup?"

"I want to pretend you don't exist so I can return to the way things were." He sounded so grumpy.

Because I rocked his world.

"The way things were was boring."

"Says who?" he replied.

"Me, because I wasn't a part of it."

He almost cracked a smile. "You are definitely not boring."

"And I taste good."

"Divine. But it means nothing."

"Afraid your buddies will tease you if they find you're dating a cat?"

"More concerned your king will decide to tear my head off and use it as a soccer ball for daring to seduce instead of protect you."

"Arik won't care if we slept together. Although, if I get hurt, he might get a teensy bit upset. And speaking of getting hurt, we've been standing out here way too long. Let's go see what's in the cave."

He shook his head. "I think we should go back. Leave right now."

"Are you serious?" At his stoic countenance, she grumbled, "You couldn't decide this before I wrecked my manicure?"

"I was being sarcastic." He almost cracked a smile. "Why would we leave now? I came here looking for something, and we might have found it. Are you coming?"

"I already did three times," she said with a snicker.

"It will be four once we solve this mystery."

"Then what are we waiting for?" She pushed past him, and almost bit her tongue as he slapped her ass. The man had a hidden naughty side, and it pleased her inordinately to see it emerging.

They slipped inside the cave, the smell of chicken, sautéed onions, and spices making her mouth water. The sounds of the jungle—cawing of birds and buzzing of insects—diminished the farther they went into the cave. Which, she realized after a bit, was more of a tunnel, the rock smoothed and yet distinctly lava born.

As proper predators, there was no need to demand silence. They automatically kept quiet, watching their steps as they made their way through the bored hole. From a distance, the pulsing beat of music haunted its way to them. There came a break in the tempo, and a voice gabbling indicated a radio playing. There was also a noticeable hum in the air and the smell of fuel, indicating the presence of a generator. They'd found more than just a simple person camping for the night.

Had they found the lair of the liotaur? Were they about to burst into his camp and catch him?

If they played their cards right and got there quick enough, then maybe they could eat his soup before dragging him back to the resort for questioning.

Reaching the end of the tunnel, they could see more clearly. Light, the kind that came from dancing flames, lit the interior of their passage. Francois flattened himself on one side of the tunnel. She took the other as they reached the opening and peeked out to see a huge cavern.

The music on the radio burst with strong drums and piano as a new set began. It muffled any possible voices. Who knew how many people were here in the heart of the volcano?

Excitement practically had her dancing. Her lioness meowed to get out.

Not yet. We need to look around more first.

A glance around the cavern showed a small slope from the cave that rolled into the bottom of the hardened lava floor, where tents were pitched. Large military grade ones.

"What is this place?" she whispered. Because this was more than just a camp for a man dressing or shifting as a lion to steal women for debauchery.

"I don't know, and I don't like it. Stick close."

As if she needed Francois protecting her.

When he went one way, she went the other and ignored his hissed, "Get back over here."

She flashed him a finger and kept going. He either trusted her or he didn't.

He passed the test, letting her do her own thing, which was kind of cool. She took that faith in her abilities to heart and made sure to peek all around, noting that they weren't truly in a cavern but an open bowl, the heart of the volcano itself.

Overhead, netting hung over part of the camp, covering a stack of crates piled to the side. The camouflage looped across, hiding what hid within from anyone flying above. The open sections didn't have much that could be easily seen from above, the dark tents probably blending in, and no one would hear anything from high above.

But why all the secrecy?

The organization of the installation had her pulling out her phone and clicking quickly, taking a multitude of images and some videos. Only as she panned around to grab a panorama did she notice more caves riddling the side of the volcano. One even had a carved arch framing it. The signs of ancient habitation occurred only on one side, with the other half of the volcano appearing unfinished and lumpy.

Perhaps there was some truth to the ancient legends about people living within the volcano. However, ancient stories didn't explain what happened here now.

She sensed a presence and whirled. Despite realizing there was no threat, Francois still got gut punched. Even a whampyr should know better than to sneak up on a lioness.

"Was that necessary?" he gasped, his body no longer big and gray but sexy and—*mine.*

"No. Gonna spank me?" she asked with a wink. When he glared, she grinned. "Don't be grumpy. I promise to kiss it better later."

"We should go."

"Did you discover something? What is this place?" she whispered.

"I don't know. Whatever it is, though, there's money behind it. There's a helicopter landing pad on the other side of that large tent. And the generators? There's two industrial-sized ones, one to run the main camp and another to run some kind of medical lab."

"A lab out here? For what?"

"I don't know. The cages were empty."

Cages? Why would someone need cages?

"They won't be empty for long." The words were spoken by someone with no scent. None at all and a stranger.

Before Stacey could whirl and act, a dart hit her in the ass.

CHAPTER SIXTEEN

EVERYONE REACTS DIFFERENTLY WHEN ATTACKED. Some drop to their knees and beg for mercy. Others cry. Some become enraged.

Only Stacey would laugh, clap her hands, and sing, "Run, run as fast as you can. I'm faster than the Gingerbread Man." And then she darted at the guy holding the tranquilizer gun. A guy whose eyes widened as she charged toward him.

JF could understand why. Fur sprouting, body changing, Stacey let her lioness come out to play.

The beautiful feline, with her russet-tinged fur, hit the ground with four feet, only she never reached the guy who shot her full of drugged darts. Three by JF's count. She slowed and wavered, the chemical cocktail strong enough to take down even a shifter.

So of course he shouted, "I told you someone darted me!"

It was, after all, a perfect "I told you so" moment.

They also tried to dart him again. But this time JF

expected it, and dodged. It occurred to him he could change forms in a blink of an eye. In his whampyr shape, he could fight with more deadly force and grace; however, the odds of winning? Not so good given at least two of the guns aimed at him had bullets that would hurt.

He had a split second to decide—go full-on whampyr and attack, see just how good fighters the three men surrounding them were, or play the part of weakling and see what was truly going on.

Seeing Stacey collapse, the drugs working quickly on her, decided him. He couldn't risk her getting hit in the crossfire. Nor did he dare change when he still had no idea what he faced. The two men with guns trained on him had no scent. None at all. Were they whampyr like him? He couldn't tell, especially since they didn't bear any marks on their skin.

Staring at them meant he didn't dodge the dart aimed at his back. The drugs invaded his system, and he felt a slight lethargy. Only slight. His body had already learned to adapt from his last dosage. A whampyr trait that protected them from poisons.

They won't take me down so easily again.

A part of him wanted to smile, the cold beast within eager to play. Except he wanted to know more before he tore off any heads. Decapitated bodies didn't speak very well.

So JF sank to his knees slowly and then managed to collapse so that he at least partially covered Stacey.

Someone who wanted them dead wouldn't bother with a sleeping agent, but it didn't hurt to be cautious with her.

As to when he started to give a fuck what happened

to her...perhaps he should blame it on a spider bite or something in the food. He didn't know when or how or why it occurred, and yet he felt something for the woman. Something more than just hunger or lust. An emotion that overcame the anger at his past.

Who cared if a lioness had betrayed him a long time ago?

Did it matter if they were so different?

She's mine.

So why wasn't he going beast mode on these ambushing bastards?

Because sometimes caution was the better part of valor.

Stifling the monster within that wanted to feed, he let himself go completely limp and didn't react when hands pulled at him, lifting him. JF heard their surprise.

"He's not as heavy as he looks," said Doofus Number One.

Well duh. Heavy bodies were harder to fly.

"She is," grumbled Doofus Number Two.

Stacey wasn't heavy. Just solid. And whoever complained was lucky she slept because he'd wager money that kind of remark would see someone disemboweled.

"What the fuck is she wearing?" asked Doofus One.

"I don't know, but my girlfriend could probably make a fortune on stage wearing it."

We should feast on their eyeballs. Playing the part of sleeping victim was all well and good, but if they dared to start stripping his princess, all bets were off.

They weren't carried too far, the rustle of canvas indicating they'd entered a tent. Given he'd done a quick scout, JF was not too surprised to hear the rattle of metal.

Hitting the ground hard, the thin blanket covering it not a true cushion, he could now state with certainty that he knew the purpose of the cages. JF could smell the scent of those who'd passed before, such as the woman who'd just been recovered.

Slam. Click.

His cage shut behind him, but he didn't hear a second click, indicating the other one had locked Stacey up.

"She's awful pretty," muttered the second Doofus.

Yup, definitely eating his eyeballs first.

"You know what the boss said about touching the merchandise. We can't leave any traces on them."

"I've got gloves."

Then he'd eat his hands.

"I guess if we use a rubber..."

That was quite enough. JF's lip peeled back as he prepared to act, only a sharp rebuke, "Touch her and I'll cut your dick off myself," stopped him.

He knew that voice, but usually it simpered.

"We were just kidding, boss."

Boss?

"Get out of here. Now," was the barked order. "Get ready. We've got a chopper arriving for a shipment in the next fifteen minutes."

Shipment of what?

"On it." Followed by a rustle of canvas and a muttered, "Bossy bitch."

Silence fell with only the hum of machines filling the air. Breathing in through his nose didn't indicate any scent other than Stacey's. Were they alone?

He pried open an eyelid to find a pair of familiar blue eyes staring at him.

"Hello, Jean Francois. I am surprised you came for a visit so soon after this afternoon."

Since the gig was up, he sat and looked Jan in the eye. "What's going on here?"

"Science. The medical wave of the future."

"What kind of science? What are you doing taking people prisoner?"

"Is this the part where I'm supposed to launch into a villainous monologue about how my shitty childhood made me turn to a life of crime?"

"It would help." But wasn't necessary. There were only two real reasons people committed crimes. Money, which went hand in hand with power, or passion. Since he didn't know Jan, and he doubted Jan knew the other guests, he doubted passion had anything to do with her actions. Especially given the clinical nature of the equipment in the tent.

"Let's just say you and your so-called sister in the cage over there have something people will pay dearly for. And I am in the perfect position to provide it."

"Experiments on your own kind?"

"My kind?" She snorted. "I am nothing like the animals I put in these cages."

At that, he frowned and sniffed. Frowned some more. "Where is your scent?"

"I have none, courtesy of a special cologne." She smiled. "It's called nothing. As in not human, not shifter, nothing. It comes in an aerosol, and it's very popular with the mercenary groups."

"So you're using the people you capture to develop a non-scent?"

"Of course not. The recipe for it is actually based on a flower that grows only in a few volcanoes. But this is my favorite place to collect it, given the Lleyoniias were kind enough to leave the instructions to the nothing scent behind in this one."

"If you use plants to make it, then why the cages? Why capture Shania and those other girls that went missing?"

Jan's expression brightened into an Aha moment. "So you *are* here to investigate. I thought so. You and that woman failed at the whole sibling thing."

Probably because he couldn't keep his hands or eyes off Stacey. "You won't get away with whatever you're doing. People have begun to notice the odd happenings on this island."

"Then I guess we'll have to shift camps. We can get samples from the animals elsewhere if needed."

"Samples of what?"

"Blood. Semen. But the most popular thing on the market right now is eggs. Shapeshifter eggs. Did you know they can be used in a variety of medical procedures? They make the best stem cells for treatments."

"You're harvesting eggs?" From unwilling and unknowing hosts. Even he was appalled. "How can you do that to your own kind?"

"Not my kind," she spat. "What has you and all those other animals fooled is the scent I wear. Again, another recipe I found when I stumbled across a cave in the volcano."

"You're not a lion shifter." The news took him by surprise. He'd never had his nose fooled before.

"Bingo. He finally gets it. I'm surprised it took you this long. Then again, you're not a shifter either. But you are something more than human. I just haven't figured out what. What I do know is you're nothing at all like the woman." She pointed to the limp Stacey. "The blood samples we took this afternoon—"

"Where did you put the samples?" Knowing she'd taken some of his blood brought a chill, mostly because the first rule Gaston made him learn after his creation was to never let anyone keep his blood. There were secrets in his blood. Secrets the world couldn't find out.

"Aren't you just the demanding one. In case you hadn't noticed, you're in the cage, which makes you the prisoner."

"You can't keep me here."

"Oh, but I can. These bars are silver imbued and shifter resistant."

As if he cared. He'd escaped worse places than this. "What are you planning to do with us?"

"After we take some more samples, we wipe your memories and put you back, none the wiser."

"I won't forget."

"You'd better hope you do because otherwise you will die. A tragic accident in paradise. Happens all the time with the tourists." Her smile proved quite cunning.

For some reason, it made him brash. "I can see why Stacey hates you. You are a sly bitch."

"And you have a really unhealthy relationship with your sister."

"On account she's not my sister, and you messed with

the wrong people." He stood, his shoulders brushing the top of the cage.

And still Jan smirked, thinking she held the upper hand. "Do your worst. We had a bear shifter in here a month ago, big bastard, and he couldn't even bend the bars."

"But I'm not a shifter," he growled as he let the beast rise, the skin on his body turning dark, his teeth elongating, and his wings popping free. He didn't stop at his hybrid shape either. Despite knowing a lack of feeding would leave him weak, he kept on shifting, his body thickening, horns spiraling from his forehead. His breaths emerged in a puff of smoke.

Goggling him, Jan didn't retreat. The stupid woman still didn't understand she now breathed her last.

Soon she would grasp just how badly she'd fucked up when she chose to mess with him.

JF grabbed hold of the bars, hearing the hiss of skin being crisped by the silver alloy in them. He didn't care. He pulled, and at first, nothing happened, and Jan's shocked look turned into a smirk.

Then there was a creak. A groan of metal bending and her eyes widened as the bars began to twist. A whampyr who let the beast through all the way was not restricted by the laws of physics when it came to strength but, rather, could call on magic, that ethereal force that bound all living things, and use it. Use it to enhance his strength and will. Not for long, not without blood to fortify him, but long enough to break free of this puny cage.

At last Jan realized her mistake. "Someone get in here

with a gun!" Jan shouted. Silly girl. She should have instead started running. He did so like to chase.

JF was done playing opossum. *I am not a prisoner or a mere mortal to be trifled with.*

He was better than her. Better than anyone. And he had to act now, destroy the blood she'd stolen. Destroy her before she could reveal any of his secrets.

In the distance, he heard the whirring of a chopper. Would it carry reinforcements?

Best take care of those in camp now.

Time to hunt.

He slid through the gap he'd made in the bars, and finally Jan moved, running from the tent shouting for help. "Someone shoot him!"

She called for a rain of bullets. Painful, but not deadly. Not unless they blew up his head.

While the front entrance beckoned, he avoided it. No point in making himself a target. He shot straight up, claws extended to tear himself an opening in the roof of the tent. He balanced on the metal pole ridge holding the canvas up, using it for a short moment before launching himself into the sky, the screams by Jan, the shouts of the men, and the loudening roar of the chopper making for chaos. The best kind of distraction for a stealthy creature of the night.

Swooping from the sky, the man JF slammed into never saw him coming. He used the other male as a cushion for his landing, his knee ramming hard in the spine, his hands grasping him by the head and twisting.

Crack.

One down. No mercy. Leaving them behind meant

possibly facing them again later at a less opportune moment.

JF scooped the rifle and took once again to the skies, holding himself aloft with mighty pulls of his wings, hearing the roar of the chopper as it began its descent into the bowl, and the wind caught at his wings. He alighted on a ledge, the slim rocky shelf enough room for him to balance and take aim at a man running toward the tent holding the cage and Stacey.

Oh no you don't.

Pop.

His shot took down the fellow, and Jan screamed more in rage than anguish.

The chopper landed, and he took aim at it, the shot ricocheting off the whirring blades. A pair of men poured out of it, armed and ducking immediately behind objects for cover.

Since JF found himself exposed, he took to the skies and might have enjoyed himself picking them off, except someone had the brilliant idea of turning on a huge spotlight, the same one they'd lit for the helicopter to land and aimed it upwards—which explained the rumors he'd heard from staff about the strange lights in the sky. People preferred to believe in the inexplicable rather than search out the truth.

The bright beam caught him, and a bullet soon followed the heat of its passage, narrowly missing his wing.

He dipped and swirled, looking for openings. But there were several of them firing blindly into the sky, making it difficult for him to attack.

A smarter whampyr might have taken off. After all,

he was no longer caged; he was free to go. Leave. Save himself.

Saving himself, though, meant leaving Stacey behind. He wouldn't even contemplate it. If he left, then it would be because she came with him.

And then there was the fact they still had his blood.

I'm not going anywhere. Not until he'd taken care of business.

He fired and heard someone yelp. Then he was the one hissing in pain as a bullet finally tore into him, grazing his wing, but it distracted him, caused him to falter, and another bullet tore through the paper-thin parchment-like skin, upsetting his balance.

Since the sky was no longer his friend, he dropped, hitting the ground feet first with a hard thump. He fell into a crouch and tucked his wings close, feeling the throb of the hole as flesh knitted together, the hot thrill of blood coursing through his veins.

The beast inside pulsed and pushed, begging to fully come out. Few knew it, but the form JF usually morphed into was a hybrid version of his whampyr. There existed a deeper, darker part of him still.

Don't wake the monster. Because once woken, only blood would appease.

Men with guns, led by a smirking Jan, converged. "Don't kill him. I want some more samples first."

JF let them get close, his head bowed, the picture of subservience. Broken, bleeding, and beaten.

Or so they thought. He still had one more trick up his whampyr sleeve.

When they got within reach, he smiled, wickedly and without mirth, as he pulled at the world around him, sucked at everything he could find in the air and the ground. His horns tingled, storing all that sweet power. When he was full to the brim, he grabbed it and thrust it out of him in a dark cloud, a fog of night so deep no light could penetrate.

But he didn't need to see to hunt.

As a shield, it did wonders, but he couldn't use it for long, and so he moved quickly, tracking by sound. A whimper, a scuff of shoes, panting breath. His teeth snapped at his prey, gnashing their flesh, releasing blood, blood that he drank. He guzzled it the hot coppery fluid, feeding the monster that hungered. Replenishing the leeching strength from his big body.

When the fog dissipated, it was to see bodies on the ground, broken and torn. Eyes staring sightlessly. His enemies vanquished while he pulsed with power.

I want more.

He looked around and noticed a particular body was missing.

"Where are you, Jan?" He was still feeling peckish.

The fact that she wore the nothing scent made it easy for him to follow her. It was the one path that negated everything around it. It led to the far side of the crater, the open area marked for landing.

The chopper hadn't wasted time. While some men might have joined the hunt, others loaded the chopper. The stack of crates nearby was gone, and the big metal bird was leaving. At the window, Jan's pale face peeked, a middle finger pressed against the glass in a final salute.

Good riddance. He'd had quite enough of her.

She raised her other hand and waved a familiar belt.

Stacey's utility belt.

Bitch took my princess.

The beast consumed him at that point, roared through him, pulsing and bursting every atom he had left.

Unleashing a mighty bellow, he shot off after the chopper.

His wings flapped, hard, and yet he was no match for a machine. The helicopter drew away from him, taking not only his enemy but also his woman out of reach.

Frustration made him scream, the primal sound of rage echoing around the inside of the volcano, so loud the very walls vibrated.

He cried out again.

Rumble. Another tremor rocked the volcano's inner lining.

Rock cracked.

Crumbled.

A large chunk from the lip dropped and hit the chopper, mangling a blade. The metal bird began to list drunkenly in the air, losing altitude, and JF arrowed toward it, willing himself to move faster.

He couldn't move fast enough. The helicopter slammed into the side of the volcano, and something ignited.

A whoosh of flames engulfed the chopper, so quickly and fiercely that the screams lasted only seconds before dying out. Before everything inside that chopper died.

The burning heap of metal plummeted, as did his heart. He sank more slowly to the ground, staring in horror at the wreckage. A smoldering ruin with no survivors.

She's dead. I killed her.

He shouldn't have cared.

Princess...

No.

No. No. No. A hole gaped in chest, and he yelled as he pounded at himself.

Only as the echo died away, leaving behind only the snapping crackle of flames, did he hear it far off in the distance.

A piercing shriek.

CHAPTER SEVENTEEN

REGAINING CONSCIOUSNESS, on a bare shoulder —drooling only a little bit—wasn't the most awful thing that ever happened to Stacey. The time she woke up hugging the outhouse that had seen too many chili incidents? Still made her shudder.

She'd also woken to much uglier views than that of the cute little butt flexing in the thong flossing the cheeks.

However, she should note it wasn't JF's butt waggling. Nor was it his body that carted Stacey through the lava tunnel. And the hair tickling her was most definitely dead.

"Oh gross, are you seriously wearing a lion's mane?" she exclaimed.

Maurice huffed and puffed as he replied. "You're not supposed to be awake."

"I'm sorry. Did your date rape drug wear off?" She had a high tolerance. Most of her biatches did. Blame the drinking. Blame their teenage rebellious years. Some older pride scientists said something about their shifter genes metabolizing things more quickly. Whatever. It meant Maurice had miscalculated.

"I'm not the one who drugged you. My sister did."

Sister, as in Jan. The plot thickened. Not really. She'd kind of figured they were related. They had the same sly eyes.

"Your sister might have ordered those tranqs, and yet here you are carting me off wearing butt floss and a dead animal on your head."

"I'm saving you." Said with the kind of attitude that indicated Maurice expected praise.

"From what?"

"From the battle."

"I'm missing a battle for this?" She craned to look back, but the twists and turns of the tunnel meant she couldn't see a thing. Well, that sucked. She would have enjoyed hitting some things. Then again, the night waned young and she was being abducted. There was still hope someone would die, or at the very least sob for his mommy.

"Don't worry. I have a place for us to go to stay safe. It's not far."

Better not be because the way Maurice was huffing, he might pass out before then. It was enough to give a girl a complex. Except she knew JF could carry her without problem.

Emerging from the tunnel, not the same one they'd used to get in, they found themselves in a new part of the jungle, the clearing well-trodden, the rock walls around it penning her in as surely as a palisade. No easy escape.

For Maurice.

Good. Stacey felt an urge to speak with the boy, and at least out here, no one would hear him scream.

Maurice set her down, and she spent a moment looking around, the sheer rock walls unrelieved black stone but for the tunnel they'd emerged from. To the far edge of the rather large clearing, the ground mostly trampled dirty with a few scrubby plants struggling to push up, sat a hut, rough logs strapped together with a thatched roof.

"What's this?"

"My secret place. There's a bed inside," he advised.

"You brought me to your love shack?"

"I prefer to call it the temple of conception."

That caused her to turn around to stare at him. "Your what?"

"The temple. You'll soon see. I shall bless you like I blessed the others."

Maurice was the liotaur on the video. A fake one. Not only that. *There's something wrong with him.* Her nose twitched. Her inner lioness paced.

Smells wrong.

Which made no sense. On the one hand, Maurice smelled like a lion, the stench of it overwhelming, and yet...something seemed off about it. Almost as if the scent was false.

Then there was the hat he wore. No self-respecting shifter, of any caste, would be caught dead wearing a deceased animal.

"Isn't there an unspoken rule that we don't wear our ancestors, even if they're not as evolved as us?" she asked.

"I am more than a mere shifter." Maurice puffed out

his chest, the lean lines of it attractive but not as sexy as the bulk of a certain whampyr. "I am a god."

She couldn't help it. She laughed.

No surprise, he took offense. "Stop it. I am a god. I'll have you know my family is descended from the Lley-oniias tribe."

"If you're a god, then prove it. Shift instead of wearing a dead fur hat."

"I don't have to prove anything."

At that, she let out a disdainful snort. "Because you can't. You're wasting my time."

She went to move around him, but Maurice blocked her. She thought about shoving him flat onto his ass. It wouldn't take much effort.

"I command you to go into the temple and drink the sacred wine. All will become clear once you do."

Want to bet he'd laced it? "I am not drinking your wine."

"You're being stubborn."

"It's called being a woman. Which maybe you'd know if you didn't have to drug all your dates to get some action."

"I didn't drug all of them. Most came with me quite willingly."

"And returned remembering nothing. Why is that? Afraid they'd talk about your teeny tiny weenie?" Her pointed stare at his loincloth might have shrunk it further.

"I am a great lover. And if it wasn't for the project—"

She interrupted. "What project?" Exactly what had she missed during her impromptu nap?

"The one my sister started. The project to sell scents

and shifter stem cells, and even ovum, to the black market."

"There's a market for my eggs?" She stared down at her stomach with a frown. "So that's what's been going on? Dude, you are so dead. Stealing eggs and stuff without permission is not cool. My king is going to rip you a new one." Right after Stacey slapped him around for a little while for being an asshat.

"Your king won't find me. Not without a scent." Maurice pulled a vial from his loincloth—just more proof he didn't hide any major junk under it—and spritzed himself. He went from obnoxious-smelling lion to...

"Nothing. Holy poop on a cracker." Stacey might have said more, but an explosion rocked the world hard enough to vibrate the ground underfoot. A faint smell of smoke came from the tunnel, but of more interest was the primal cry of rage that followed.

Want to bet someone just discovered her missing? And boy did he sound upset.

It brought a smile to her lips. "You're in so much trouble now." And then, it didn't take much effort, none at all given she could just imagine all the hairy things crawling all around her, to let out a shriek to end all shrieks.

"Stop that!" Maurice yelled. He lunged at her, but she danced out of reach.

She could have taken care of him. Easily too. But she had a feeling someone might need a little stress relief.

Maurice dove at her again, this time aiming a needle —one thing more pulled from his tiny loincloth.

"Mickey me once, shame on me, mickey me again, and my boyfriend will tear your head off," she sang.

The stupid human, who styled himself as something more, paused as a shadow covered him.

Alighting with a grace that belied his monstrous appearance, Francois joined the party, his big bat appearance now more on par with a gargoyle. The horns curling from his forehead were a nice touch. As for the smoke coming from his nostrils?

Epic.

"About time you saved me." Stacey crossed her arms and tossed her hair.

Francois, a cross between a gargoyle and a demon at this point, grunted.

Maurice, on the other hand, squeaked like a mouse and ran.

Never run in front of a predator.

Ever.

Might as well put a sign on that said, "Eat me."

Maurice disappeared into the tunnel, his hairy hat bobbing; whereas, Francois took to the sky.

Tapping her foot, Stacey waited. It didn't take long to hear the scream.

A scream cut short.

Moments later, the big-winged beast landed in front of her, smoke puffing from his nostrils, his eyes red.

"Took you long enough."

A growl rolled out of him as he reached for her with big hands, the fingers tipped in claws. Yet he was gentle with her, drawing her close and sniffing her. The smoky aroma of his musk surrounded her, and his leather skin had an unexpected softness. He nuzzled her hair before pressing his mouth against her neck.

She closed her eyes and sighed. "Isn't this nice? You and me, alone in the jungle."

He snorted, a sound that turned into a laugh as he transformed. "You almost get killed and you call it romantic?"

"Please. I could have handled Maurice. But, given I am a princess, it was only right that my hero come to my rescue."

"I'm no hero."

"And yet you're here. Does that mean you don't want the hero kiss?"

"Shouldn't we instead be calling for help? In case you didn't notice, we broke up a criminal ring running out of the volcano that was using your resort as a store to harvest shifter genes."

"It's been happening for months, and by the sound and smell of it, you handled it. So what's another fifteen minutes going to do?"

"Fifteen?"

"You're right." She cupped his face to draw it down. "The way I'm feeling right now, I'll only need ten, maybe even only five minutes to come."

"You can't order me around, princess." That was what he said, and yet he still fisted her hair. The sharp tug made her breath catch.

"Would you prefer me to beg?"

His free arm wrapped around her waist, drawing her buttocks back, nestling into the hollow of his groin. The hardness of his cock pressed. "I think you need to stop talking."

"Or else what?"

His fingers found the flap in her suit, the one for her

tail, which, if tugged just right, opened up the entire crotch area.

"You wouldn't want to distract me from what I plan to do." He slid his fingers into her, and she sucked in sharply at the rapidness of his penetration.

"And what do you want to do?" she asked, her query rather breathy.

"You," he whispered before grasping her earlobe in his teeth.

She moaned and sagged in his grip. "There's a bed in yonder hut," she suggested.

"Too far," he growled against her skin. "Put your hands on the wall."

By wall he meant the rock, and she palmed it, the sharp edges biting but not enough to cool her ardor as he slid his fingers back and forth against her. Feeling her slickness. Using it to rub her clit.

"Yes," she hissed.

"How is it I want you again?"

How indeed? Did it even matter?

The tip of his cock suddenly pressed at her slit, taking the place of his fingers, thick and ready to penetrate.

He angled her farther back, presenting her ass, so that he could sheath himself.

Oooh.

Yes.

Deeper.

She must have spoken aloud because he murmured, "As deep as you need." And he gave her more, the first thrusts penetrating her and hitting a sweet spot inside, the bumping friction triggering something inside her. Something powerful and all consuming.

She screamed when she came. Screamed and clawed at the stone as he kept thrusting over and over, filling her up. Stretching her.

Until he came too. The heat of his cream branding her, the touch of his mouth on her neck marking her. Her skin piercing easily at the pressure of his teeth.

Their bodies joined.

Their hearts raced as one.

A sweet and sensual moment that could have been so much more if some cock blockers had better timing.

"I told you that biatch was fine. And hot damn, who's the hunk giving her the meat?"

Stacey growled, "Mine."

CHAPTER EIGHTEEN

IT HAD BEEN two weeks since JF had fled the jungle.

Two long fucking weeks since he'd last touched or seen Stacey.

An eternity.

It wasn't as if he didn't know where she was. She'd returned from the island two days ago, having chosen to remain with the rest of her crew—who suddenly decided they needed to work on their tans, or so they claimed during the chaos that followed—as they sifted the remains of the camp. Yes, he'd kept fucking tabs on the case. Not that there was much left to discover. The fire from the helicopter had spread and destroyed most of the evidence. With Jan gone, the main link to the smuggling and other products, one could only hope they'd eradicated the threat. And now at least the shifters were forewarned and could keep a watchful eye.

Things could return to normal.

JF had fled before all that, though. Run back home

with his wings tucked. He couldn't stay, and it wasn't as if she needed him anymore.

I do. He starved without her near. Not just because he craved her blood; it went deeper than that. His soul, his very essence, mourned her absence.

He'd surely get over it. A little distance was all he needed. He managed to get away from her, and yet not one second went by that she didn't fill his thoughts. That he didn't crave her. It put him in a rather permanently shitty mood, shittier even than usual.

His boss remarked on it from their control booth overlooking the club, a club they'd had to relocate after a fire had destroyed the last one.

"You know, most people come back from a tropical paradise with a tan and a smile."

"I hate the sun." Hated even more the fact that the world around him had lost all color. His life had returned to normal—dull, gray, and meaningless. The last time it happened, a woman had betrayed him. Left him for dead.

This time...*I'm the reason for my own misery.* He'd left. Not Stacey.

When those crazy lionesses had barged in on him and Stacey in the jungle, joking and eyeing him, some even taking pictures, he'd eyed the chaos that surrounded them with horror.

What had he been thinking? Not only had he drunk from Stacey, slaked his thirst like a man in a desert, he'd allowed himself to become attached to her.

Attached to a woman who would bring noise and more felines into his life.

Was he insane?

In that moment of clarity, he'd slipped away. With

the pride on site, ready to take over the scene of the crime, and surround Stacey, he was no longer needed.

So he fled. Fled and hid like a fucking coward from the one woman who made him feel truly alive. A woman who wanted to shake up his sterile world.

It was for the best, and maybe eventually he'd believe it.

"By the way, I will need you on the floor tonight," Gaston remarked. "Reba's throwing a bachelorette party for one of her friends."

"Which means cats." He made a face.

"I prefer to think of them as our friends and allies."

"Why couldn't you be like other rich dudes and get a dog?" JF grumbled as he exited the office. For a moment, he stood at the top of the stairs, staring over at the sea of heads.

Busy night tonight. Then again, every night rocked and rolled. Ever since Reba had started dating Gaston, the entire cryptid community now seemed to think the club was their spot for partying.

The hard techno beat pulsing from the speakers washed over him, making it impossible to hear. But then again, he didn't need to hear. He could feel. Awareness prickled his skin.

She's near. A connection he wanted to deny existed between them.

His gaze scanned the room, but so much movement and color proved distracting, not enough, though, to prevent him from locating *her.*

Standing poised at the top of the stairs, he stared. Stacey looked as ravishing as ever. She made her way through the crowd of patrons, dressed in peacock colors, the dress a bright turquoise trimmed with gold, blues, and green. Her fiery hair was swept upwards and bound with a ribbon, revealing her lithe neck—a fucking tease to someone like him. Coming out of the top of the bun, peacock feathers that bounced.

I wouldn't mind seeing her bounce atop me. Lust grabbed him, fast and furious.

The tight bustier that cinched in at the waist flared over the hips, and peeking from beneath that, a tiny tutu skirt. At the back trailed a scarf of striated peacock colors.

Only Stacey had the type of confidence to wear such a thing and look delectable.

In one hand, she held a tray upon which sat glasses, several of them in various pastel shades. There were also a few fluted glasses holding red wine. Her other hand balanced another tray with smaller shot glasses filled with clear liquid. The sliced lemons gave away the tequila part.

Lots of booze. She planned to get wild.

I don't care. Let her get wasted.

And yet he kept peeking over at the room she'd disappeared into. The room Gaston would have a stashed a private party in.

He was supposed to keep an eye. The boss said so.

Don't go in there.

Was he afraid he couldn't control himself?

Yes.

Two weeks had done nothing to curb his hunger; rather it had honed the craving. Made it burn inside.

The beast within hungered.

Before JF knew it, he stood outside the room. He

203

could hear the raucous laughter of women, lots of women, but only one with the clear silver-bell laughter.

He couldn't stop himself from glancing through the large arch, pushing past the gauzy curtains shielding the room from casual observance.

There lacked the bright flashing lights of the club proper, the lighting in here much dimmer and soft. Couches lined the walls, occupied by women, most of them golden-haired. Some sat on them, others perched on the backs. Their styles ranged from casual grunge to designer boutique with heels.

The highest heels belonged to Stacey. And they were sitting on the floor in the middle of the room. As for their owner? She and several others had discovered the fabric hanging from the ceiling. They wound themselves in it that they might do an aerial dance, coiling and uncoiling within the length of the fabric, rolling upwards and then dropping down, looking as if she would fall.

He reached forward, only to snatch his hand back.

Don't go in.

He should leave. But he couldn't. Her gaze caught his. Something electric sizzled between them.

He could almost hear her whisper.

There you are.

Something pulled at him. He took a step inside before realizing he was losing control again.

He had to be stronger.

Unable to stay here, close enough that she muddled his thoughts, he turned away and pushed through the crowd in the main room, heading for the front doors where he could let some fresh air fill his lungs. It would do him some good to clear his head.

As he exited, more patrons poured in, a gang of guys dressed to the nines in suits and dress shirts and smelling very panther-ish. Damned cats, multiplying everywhere.

One of them, a tall fellow with slicked-back hair, stopped him. "I'm here for a bachelorette party."

"Inside, back room," JF declared. He tried not to care that these men would be joining the ladies.

I thought bachelorette parties were supposed to be guy-free.

Except for the strippers.

He straightened from his slouch against the wall. A man getting naked and shaking it in front of Stacey?

He didn't care.

So why was he going back inside?

And why were there people screaming?

"Gun!"

Bang. Bang.

He heard the gunfire and went shoving back in, the flow of people escaping impeding his path.

"Get out of my way." He parted the sea of bodies, his heavy stomp separating the flow that he might cross the club.

By the time he got to the back room, where of course trouble just had to occur, there were only a few women left, felines handcuffed to the stripper poles in each corner that Gaston had installed when he relocated the club.

"What the fuck happened?" he asked, his gaze darting from face to face. All shocked. None harmed. And one missing.

"It's Stacey's ex," exclaimed Reba. "He just showed up with his crew and threatened us with guns."

"And managed to capture you all?" Seemed rather unlikely.

"Your security sucks," Luna declared.

"Don't get pissy at me because they got the drop on you," he growled. "Where's Stacey?" Because he didn't see her bright red hair anywhere.

"He took her!"

"Threatened us all with a gun if she didn't go with him."

"I think he might want to hurt her," another woman added.

What?

He might have roared the word; he wasn't too sure. He kind of lost his mind as he tore to the nearest exit door, following the scent of the panthers. Smashing into the alleyway, he noted the distant blink of red taillights. And a single feather on the ground.

The monster broke free.

CHAPTER NINETEEN

THE SLIDING GLASS door shattered as he slammed through it.

Stacey smiled. "About time you showed up." What she didn't tell him was how relieved she was he'd come. When she'd hatched the plan with her biatches, she wasn't too sure Francois would act. After all, the man had fled paradise without saying goodbye.

She'd given him space. Long enough for him to recognize the error of his ways.

He surveyed the scene and frowned. "Why is your ex-boyfriend passed out on the floor?"

"I might have conked him on the head." Stupid moron actually thought he and his crew had gotten the drop on her biatches. It was almost comical the way they'd had to restrain themselves when he burst into the party room waving his puny gun.

"So, in other words, you didn't need rescuing?"

"Nope." She shook her head. "But you do."

"What are you talking about? I'm not the one constantly in trouble."

"Exactly. You're mister play it safe and don't take risks." He'd run rather than see what happened next with Stacey.

"I take plenty of risks, or did you not hear about what happened at the volcano?"

"Would you like a medal? You know how to fight. Whoopee-de-doo. So do I and all my biatches. What about taking a risk on having a relationship with me?"

"Is that what this is about? You want me to be your boyfriend?" He crossed his arms over his impressive chest. "That's sad."

"No, what's sad is the fact you can't say Stacey, I love you and want to be with you."

He flinched. "We barely know each other."

"And? No one who starts a relationship does. It's why we date. Go out for food. Have sex. Eat some more. Have sex again."

"You don't want to be with me."

"Given this is my head and my body, I'm pretty sure I know what I want to do. "

"I can't be with you. You know why."

"Oh yes you can. So what if one cunt screwed you over? We're not all like that."

"Fine. Not all women suck. We still won't work. Have you forgotten the fact that I'm whampyr?"

"I know. Totally sexy."

"Not sexy if you think about the fact I'm no longer human."

"Neither am I." Didn't he understand she didn't

care? He was still the same person inside. The man she loved.

"I drink blood to live." He bared his teeth.

She bared hers back. "I like my steak rare. And?"

"I can never father children."

Her nose wrinkled. "Noisy little things. And don't they require like constant supervision? I'd rather not."

"You say that now, but..."

She shook her head. "If you're worried I'm going to suddenly develop some maternal gene, then forget it. If I feel an urge to play mommy for a day, I'll borrow one of my biatches' babies for a few hours. Less time if it poops." She shuddered. "I don't do diapers."

"What if I lose control with you?"

"I hope you do."

"I could—"

"Hurt me?" She laughed. "You either think too highly of yourself or not enough of me. Let me tell you right now, sweetcheeks. The only thing that will hurt me is if you don't come over here and kiss me right now."

"I don't want to." Now he just sounded stubbornly petulant.

"Yes, you do. Come here now." She pointed, and in a blink of her eyes, he was there, looming over her, his virile strength making her shiver.

"If we do this, then you need to realize that whampyr are colony people. We don't like to be alone."

"Have you met my pride? We'll be lucky to get five minutes alone. Even the best locks are no match for them."

"You still talk too much," he snapped, pulling her close. "And I must be fucking sick because I missed it."

"Because you love me," she sang.

"Shut the fuck up," he growled, taking her mouth.

The kiss proved smoking, the time apart having only honed their arousal for each other. Their frantic breaths mixed as their teeth and lips clashed. Spiraling lust had them tugging at each other's clothes.

Ripping it to shreds, not caring in their quest to be skin to skin.

His mouth left hers and trailed across her jaw, nipping along the way. He fitted his mouth over the pulse in her neck, and she moaned.

"Taste me."

"We should stop," he growled, pulling away, and through half-open eyes, she saw the sharp fangs peeking from his mouth.

Time to prove, once and for all, he didn't have to fear. She pulled him close. "Taste me," said in a husky commanding voice.

With a groan, he succumbed, the sharp prick of his teeth penetrating skin, the powerful tug as he sucked a direct line to her sex.

Her sex pulsed in time with his pulling swallows.

He drank for only a moment before releasing her skin with a moan. "Fuck me, princess, you're perfection." He kissed her again, letting her taste the copper of her blood.

It only fueled the hunger flooding her. How she needed, make that wanted, him to sink deep inside her.

She twined her fingers in his hair, opening her mouth that their tongues might mesh. A hard, thick thigh inserted itself between her legs and provided a welcome friction against her sex. The gasp she let out fluttered against his mouth.

"You drive me wild," he declared.

"Good." Because he should feel alive with her. Uncontrolled. Able to let down his guard and trust.

The kiss ended with him bending her back slightly, the angle enough that he could trail his lips down the column of her throat. Down even farther to her breasts, his mouth leaving hot trails around them. His warm breath feathered across her nipples, making her shiver. He caught one of the tight buds in his mouth, sucking it and then biting down on it gently. She felt it right down to her pussy.

She panted, her fingers curling and digging into his muscled shoulders as her hips bucked. He didn't care that she writhed and begged. His mouth never lost its latch on her nipple. He drew it farther into his mouth.

"Now," she begged.

"Are you ready?" he asked, his breath warm on her lips.

"Touch me and see."

Please touch me. It had been so long.

His fingers traveled down to that spot between her legs, rubbing across her clit, dipping into her honey.

"I want to taste."

"Later. I need you." When he hesitated, she added a soft, "Please."

He groaned as he hoisted her up. Her legs wound around his waist loosely, and she trusted him to hold her as her hands gripped his cock and guided it to her sex.

She took a moment to rub the head on her clit, her breath catching at the sensation. It had been too long, though; she couldn't wait any more. She lined up the head of his shaft and wiggled to push the head in. Then she tightened her limbs around him, drew him close, sinking his cock deep into her body.

His hands gripped her by the ass as he began to bounce her, lifting and dropping her on his cock, simple strength alone keeping her aloft. His shaft sinking deeply each time. Each slam making her pussy tighten around him, coiling her pleasure. Tightening every ounce of her being as she raced for that orgasmic peak.

And when it hit, when everything in her froze for a second before pulsing, she bit him.

Bit him hard enough to break skin. She tasted blood, heard him groan loudly, and then he was biting her too, the pair of them joined, flesh to flesh, blood to blood, soul to soul.

Forever.

And of course her stupid ex chose that moment to say, "Get your hands off my girl."

Wrong thing to say. In Francois's defense, Michael shouldn't have chosen to kidnap her and hold her prisoner on the penthouse level. They couldn't even use dental records to identify him when they scraped him off the ground, which meant no one knew who he was and what room he'd jumped from. It meant uninterrupted time, which they needed because, as soon as JF finished tossing Michael off the balcony, he turned to her and said, "You're mine."

It was one of the sexiest things anyone had ever done for her, which was why, minutes later, Francois received the best head in his life in the shower.

They didn't come out of that hotel room for five days.

New record.

EPILOGUE

"NO." He sounded so firm.

"Please," she cajoled and fluttered her lashes.

It failed to work. "Still no, princess."

"But I had it specially made." Stacey dangled the costume from her finger and grinned. Francois refused to budge.

Even after sex.

She pouted. "How are we supposed to win cutest couple at the club if you won't wear a costume?"

"I refuse to be emasculated in such a fashion. No costume."

"But the winner is supposed to receive a bottle of expensive champagne."

"I'll steal it for you."

"I could steal it myself if I really wanted it."

"Tell you what, you really want to go to this party, I will." At her smile, he added, "As myself. But I actually had a better idea for tonight." He drew her close. "Take off your panties."

Another woman might have asked why. She just pushed up her skirt and yanked them down. Hello, anything that required no panties sounded like fun.

"Now what?" she asked, anticipation making her tingle.

"Hold on tight because there's no net in the clouds."

Was it any wonder she loved this man? He might show the world a fearsome scowl. He might not laugh or smile easily, but he knew how to make her happy.

And not just because of the awesome sex several hundreds of feet above ground, but because after, he held her close and murmured, "I love you, princess."

Being a brat, she held out a camera and shouted, "Beat this bitches!" Then hashtagged it, #bejealous #soinlove #sendfoodwithdoves. Fuck it, #justsenddoves

---

A FEW WEEKS later at the pride tech division known as Melly's second bedroom...

The letter with its serious logo at the top mocked her. How dare the government think to audit her? She'd filed her taxes, claimed her expenses, and now they were asking her to justify them.

As if she needed to justify her need for a spa day after a hard week of work. Being a computer geek meant Melly spent long hours sitting. It was practically the doctor's orders that she take a day off and let someone massage and pamper her poor body. Except, apparently, she needed a doctor's note and more for some of her other deductions.

Since her creative accounting was not appreciated,

she found herself in an awkward position.

"Ahem."

Head down, ass in the air, scrabbling for the sticky note that fell out of the sheaf of papers in her hand, she peeked between her legs, upside down, at the perfectly pressed crease on the pants of the guy behind her. Obviously a human because a shifter male would have done something dirty like slap her ass or tried to hump it. He probably would have suffered a maiming as well—but only if he was gross rather than humping material.

"Who let you in?" she asked. Because she didn't recall hearing a knock or a doorbell.

"The door was wide open and no one answered when I called out."

"Are you the IRS fellow?" she asked, spotting the sticky note on the sole of her shoe. Retrieving it, she unfolded herself, not very far, as she only stood just over five feet, and looked up at the human. And up.

Standing in a suit, with an impeccably tied cravat and thick-rimmed glasses was a hot nerd.

I could totally see myself doing numbers with him. All night long. Rowr.

The End... Until Melly gets involved with an auditor for the IRS, who is much more than the geek she sees in When A Lioness Hunts.

For more arrogant shifters, and humor, try the Dragon Point Series.